a

Mistletoe

Mismatch

a mistletoe mismatch

SALLY BRITTON

Published by Pink Citrus Books
Edited by Jenny Proctor of Midnight Owl Editors
Cover design by Laura Rollins
Cover photo licensed through Arcangel

Sally Britton
www.authorsallybritton.com

First Printing: November 2021

For Shaela Kay Odd
A Woman Who Celebrates Christmas All Year Long
Merry Christmas, Dearest Friend

CHAPTER 1

December 9th, 1815

WINTER CREPT SLOWLY ACROSS THE REST OF THE COUNTRY before coming to Devonshire. Or so Jessica Nettle thought, looking out her bedroom window at the dismally gray sky. She pushed the window open, its oiled hinges not protesting in the slightest, and leaned out enough to look at the thermometer she had tacked to the window's frame.

A cold waft of air slipped by her, causing her bedroom door to slam and her younger sister to emit a tiny yelp. "You are producing a horrible draft."

After assuring herself the temperature outside was still well above freezing, though it certainly felt cold enough to make frost appear on one's nose, Jessica ducked back inside and closed the window.

"I didn't know you'd come in my room." She looked over her shoulder at her sister with an apologetic smile. Then she picked up the notebook she kept on the desk.

1

"I cannot think knowing the exact temperature is of any use. One only needs to know if one ought to wear a muff when going out of doors, and I can decide that without a thermometer." Florence came to peer out the window herself and shivered. "Do you think it will rain again?"

Florence, at nineteen years of age, was the very picture of loveliness. When she stood just so before the window, the faint light of day bathed her face in a gentle glow. With golden hair and warm brown eyes, her sister's outward beauty matched her inner gentleness. When Jessica answered, it was with fondness.

"As I have no barometer to measure air pressure rising and dropping, I cannot say." Jessica jotted down the state of the weather. "But I would certainly carry an umbrella *and* a muff. Just in case." She put the notebook away and went to her bureau. She opened the top drawer and sorted through carefully pressed shawls before finding the deep green one she favored.

Her coloring wasn't quite as striking as Florence's, and certainly didn't catch as many male gazes. Now two and twenty, Jessica's blonde hair had darkened to an indeterminate color neither yellow nor brown, and though she had blue eyes, the pupil was ringed in green. Her mother called them fairy eyes.

Florence leaned against the wall and folded her arms across her bodice. "I am worried about Aunt Tempie is all. She should have arrived yesterday." Their grandmother's sister, Mrs. Temperance Bolingbrooke, had finally agreed to spend several weeks with their family. She didn't plan to leave until after Epiphany, which meant spending the whole of Christmas together, too.

"As it rained two days past, you must see how that delay is perfectly acceptable." Jessica wrapped herself snugly in her shawl. "Papa and Mama are not concerned. Neither should you be." She took her sister by the hand. "Let us think on more cheerful things. Come downstairs with me, so we can plan where to put our boughs of green."

"It is days still before we decorate," Florence protested, though her feet followed Jessica eagerly enough. "The ribbons haven't even arrived from Boothe's yet."

The local sundries and notions shop carried ribbons throughout the year, but always ordered large spools of gold, silver, red, and green for the neighborhood to festoon their homes for the Christmas celebrations. Jessica wished, as she did every year, that the festivities began early and lasted much longer. But it simply wasn't practical to put evergreen up before Christmas Eve. The needles and holly leaves would dry out and fall every-where, creating a terrible mess for the staff.

But there was something quite magical about the house smelling of pine, the glitter of silver bells and bright red ribbon, and the glow of candles in every window. At Christmas, no matter the gray and dull weather outside, her family made merry inside with games, delicious treats, and telling stories.

An hour passed, with Jessica keeping Florence busy. She and her sister went up and down the corridors, plan-ning everything as though they didn't have tradition to rely upon when it came time to make their house ready. Most of the holly sprigs and long, green branches coming into the house would go in the usual places above mantels and around banisters. But there was always one notable exception to the family traditions.

"Where will we hide our kissing balls this year?" Florence asked, standing beneath a doorway that led into their dining room. "When will you put yours out?"

Jessica's heart gave a strange twist as an old memory tried to surface. She squelched it, as one would a beetle beneath their heel. She pulled her shawl closer. "I thought I wouldn't bother making one."

Florence spun gracefully on her slippered heel. "What? How could you not? We have made kissing balls since we were children."

Jessica feigned interested in the long-case clock, stretching her arm as though to dust off its top. "Maybe we should wrap this old thing up in silver ribbon, to brighten it up."

"Do not change the subject." Florence came closer and eyed first the clock and then her sister. "But I should think gold ribbon would be more suitable." She touched Jessica lightly on the arm. "Why would you forgo the kissing balls? You know how much Mama and Papa love them, and even Mr. and Mrs. Wilson like pretending they have forgotten where we put them." The butler and house-keeper, a married couple, always made a show of getting caught beneath the kissing balls.

"I am getting too old for such silly games. Everyone in the house knows where we put them, and then they all pretend to get caught under the Christmas balls anyway." Jessica shrugged. "Given that we are to have guests for Christmas, and you and I are of age, it might no longer be appropriate."

"Bah." Florence waved the excuses away as though

they were no more trouble than a twist of smoke. "Everyone loves mistletoe, Jessica. It is only innocent fun. If you aren't going to enjoy making yours, I suppose it is up to me to make them both *and* hide both. Then won't you be sorry when you are caught beneath one with a handsome stranger." She batted her eyelashes and pretended to swoon.

"Handsome stranger?" Jessica had to resist laughing at her sister's antics. "We know every man for twenty miles; none of them are strangers."

"But some of them are handsome," Florence countered. "Like Mr. Thackery."

"Mr. Thackery?" Jessica's chin jerked upward. "Our neighbor? He's as old as father."

For an odd moment, Florence's cheeks turned pink. "No, no. His son. Franklin Thackery."

"Frank?" Jessica shuddered. "I have known him entirely too long to see him as something other than the fixture that he is. Franklin Thackery is dull and tiresome. All he ever talks about is flora and fauna." She walked away from the clock, her sister, and hopefully all ideas of creating kissing boughs.

Florence hurried to keep up, tucking her hands behind her back as they walked toward the front door. "An interest in the natural world isn't necessarily dull. People could say the same thing about your thoughts on travel. All you ever do is talk about places you have never been."

Though her sister did not speak intending to harm, Jessica felt a pinprick of hurt nonetheless. Their elder brother, Jonathan, was away at that very moment. In Greece. He'd gone away to study architecture, and he wrote them long letters of all he saw. He often bemoaned the state of old buildings and antiquities that Napoleon had ordered removed or destroyed.

Jonathan would return home in the spring. Jessica could only hope he would bring more of the far-away world home for her to examine and discover.

"I didn't know my geographical interests bored you so," she said, trying to sound unaffected by the familiar longing. A longing to take off running down the road and go as far as it would take her. Instead, she stayed at home on her family's estate. Never venturing farther than Watford for large assemblies or concerts.

She hadn't ever even set foot in London. Not because their family couldn't afford such a trip. But because her parents had no inclination to leave their cozy home and friendly neighbors.

"I am thoroughly interested in anything you have to say, as a devoted younger sister must be." Florence linked her arm with Jessica's, smiling fondly. "I wish to convey that not everyone can be interested in the same topics or hobbies. That is all."

Before Jessica could respond, they both froze where they stood at the familiar sounds of carriage wheels and horse hooves on the drive. Jessica and Florence looked at each other, then they hurried for the front door as if they were children of five and nine again, welcoming their great aunt with enthusiasm.

Florence arrived at the door first and threw it open before running outside, though she wasn't at all dressed for the brisk weather. A fine coach and four came to a stop on the gravel before the front door. The coachman atop the box started shouting commands to the two grooms with him.

One of the grooms, dressed warmly against the weather, opened the door of the box and put his hand inside.

A hand clad in a velvety black glove took his, and down from the carriage stepped a woman with graying hair and snapdragon green eyes. Aunt Temperance Bolingbrooke carried herself with the same regal grace as a duchess, despite her sixty-odd years. She wore a black bonnet trimmed in dyed silk flowers, and a gown of deep purple trimmed in black lace, with a coat to match.

"My darlings," she crooned when she saw them standing there, holding their breath and watching her with the same awe they had held when they were much younger. When she had come to visit on the arm of her husband, an architect. He had died six months before, due to a complaint of the heart. But there had been no doubt in Jessica's young mind that the couple had loved each other dearly and had treasured each adventure they undertook together.

Florence again moved first, throwing her arms around their great aunt with enthusiasm. "Aunt Tempie, I was so worried when you didn't arrive as planned."

Aunt Temperance returned the embrace and bestowed a kiss on Florence's cheek. "And yet, here I am. Perfectly at ease and eager for my visit to Brookfield House." She turned to look at the maid who had stepped out of the carriage behind her. "Florence, be a good girl and take Mutton's basket from Harper."

Harper, the maid, handed the hamper she held to Florence at once. An excited little yelp came from inside.

Florence crooned at the small dog inside the basket.

"Oh, poor thing. Let me take him to the garden so he can stretch out a bit."

"Thank you, my dear." Then Aunt Temperance turned her full gaze upon Jessica, and her eyes glowed with affection. "My darling Jess. Were you worried for me, too?" She put her arms out, and Jessica hurried to step into the comforting embrace.

"How could I worry?" she asked, snuggled into her great-aunt's soft fur collar. "You have climbed pyramids and mountains, crossed oceans and rivers. Driving in a coach from one county to another isn't even going to fatigue you."

The older woman laughed, tucking Jessica's arm through hers. "I did all those things when I was much younger, my dear. Nearer your age." They walked up the steps together, and just before they walked through the door a tiny dog with a silky white coat darted between their legs and into the house.

Florence ran up behind them, panting. "He's a fast one."

"Indeed." Aunt Temperance's laugh burst out brightly. "He is a terror of a terrier, as my dear Henry used to say."

"We were so sorry to hear about Uncle Henry's death," Jessica said, her voice lowered now that they were inside the house.

"I am afraid it took me by surprise," Aunt Tempie said. She stripped off her gloves and handed them to the waiting maid, then her coat and hat. "Harper, do go fetch something warm to eat and drink for yourself, and send one of the household staff to the blue drawing room." She led her nieces with confidence, as comfortable in their house as she acted in her own.

Jessica studied her great aunt for signs of distress or weariness, but the older woman had as cheerful a disposition as Jessica had ever seen upon her face. "What have you girls been doing this morning? And you must tell me all about the planned festivities."

Before either Jessica or Florence could speak, their mother burst into the room, and all conversation turned to updating one another on family and acquaintances. Florence sat on the edge of her chair, wearing her usual look of peaceful serenity. Jessica settled in more comfortably, drinking in her aunt's fine appearance and her mother's good cheer. Aunt Tempie was Mother's favorite, too.

With the daily dip in temperature, the warmth of the approaching holiday promised days full of laughter and cozy evenings by the fire. Aunt Tempie's presence, in addition to their usual neighbors and guests, made everything perfect.

Or...almost perfect. Jessica had yet to hear if one of the neighborhood's Christmas visitors would make his usual appearance. If Mr. Webb visited his cousin, as he had nearly every year for the past two decades, she already knew precisely how to handle him.

Let Mr. Webb just *try* to ruin her enjoyment of the winter festivities. She would take great pleasure in putting him in his place. As she did every year. And this time, she would be the victor in their little game.

CHAPTER 2

A Week Later - December 17th, 1815

ELLIS WEBB HAD NO INTENTION OF MISSING CHRISTMAS with his cousin, even if the weather wasn't cooperating for his journey. The torrential rain caused two nasty delays, as well as a mud-caked carriage; the wet, coupled with the low temperatures, made him cross.

When his carriage finally arrived at Lamblyn Court, home to the Thackery family these three generations past, his mood brightened considerably. He opened the carriage himself, rather than wait for a servant's help, and dashed up the steps before the butler even opened the door.

Franklin Thackery met him in the entry hall, a wide grin on his face. "Webb, here you are at last. You are dashed late, you know."

Ellis accepted his cousin's hand with a firm shake. "Couldn't be helped. The weather threw every possible blockade into our path." He shrugged out of his overcoat, then removed his hat to hand it to a waiting footman. "Take me someplace warm, before I turn into an icicle."

"You sound like an old man in need of shawls and hot bricks." Franklin gestured to a nearby doorway. "Come this way, Grandfather, and I'll set you to rights."

Ellis made to shove his oldest and dearest friend out of the way, but Franklin dodged him and went ahead to open the door, laughing all the while. Ellis smirked as he trailed behind his cousin and breathed a sigh of relief the moment he stood before the roaring fire in the downstairs sitting room. He held out to his hands, warming them.

"Where is everyone?" Ellis asked, casting his eyes about the room. Nothing had changed in that room since his aunt had died a decade before. Given that only men lived in the Thackery house since then, it didn't surprise him. A widower with four sons likely never spared a thought for decoration.

"They gave up on you and went to church, as any good Christian must." Franklin, having already called for tea, dropped leisurely into one of the large chairs near the fire. "I volunteered to play at being heathen, though it comes at significant cost, I assure you."

"Ah, have I put your immortal soul in jeopardy?" Ellis took the chair opposite his cousin. "My apologies. I will address the matter with heaven when the time comes." He tipped his head back against the chair and closed his eyes. "Sitting in a chair that doesn't move is paradisaical in itself."

Franklin chuckled but said nothing else for so long a stretch that Ellis had to crack an eye open to be sure his friend hadn't fallen asleep. What he saw made Ellis sit upright again, at full attention. Franklin stared into the fire with an intense frown, his brow puckered, his hands clenching the arms of the chair.

"Something the matter, Frank?"

The other man blinked and shook his head. "No. That is—I'm not certain. But I have no wish to burden you with my troubles. Not when you've barely arrived."

With a wave, Ellis dismissed that concern. "Contrary to what you think, I am not an invalid in need of coddling. Tell me what has you looking grim. Then I will tell you it is all nonsense, and that you have no need to worry. At that point in the conversation, we may move on to pleasanter topics. Such as what your overly ambitious cook is serving for dinner this evening."

The cook at Lamblyn Court made delicious meals but would often forgo a tried-and-true recipe to attempt a completely foreign dish she had heard of from dubious connections. Including recipes given to her by an impish young neighbor, who always insisted she knew Ellis's *favorite* things to eat.

Jessica Nettle.

"It's Florence Nettle," Frank blurted at nearly the same moment Ellis thought of his genteel tormenter.

Ellis leaned forward, his hands gripping the arms of his chair. "I beg your pardon. What did you just say?"

Franklin turned a miserable countenance to Ellis, a weary shadow to his eyes. "Miss Florence Nettle. She causes my distraction."

Though Ellis had visited his cousin most summers of his youth, and every Christmas for so long as he could remember, he had given little attention to the younger of the two Nettle sisters. Though if quiet little Florence had grown to be as much of a rapscallion as her elder sister, he could see why that would drive a man to distraction.

Jessica Nettle had a way of twisting a man's words and actions to suit her own interpretations, and the woman had a tendency toward impishness in her pranks. He had the sneaking suspicion she planned them out well in advance, then set to her work as a general might set his soldiers upon a battlefield.

"Then I fail to see how waiting here for me has harmed you, given that you have likely avoided a run-in with Miss Florence at church or on the path to its door."

"No, you don't understand." Franklin groaned and rubbed at the circles under his eyes. "I *want* to see her. By waiting here for you, I have deprived myself of encountering her in church this day."

Bewildered, Ellis sat back and eyed his friend with confusion. "And that upsets you? You are making no sense, Frank."

"I haven't told anyone about this," Franklin pronounced, coming to his feet and stomping away to the window. "You were meant to be the first. I wished to solicit your help. But if I cannot make myself understood, how do I have any hope at all?"

Though no one had ever accused Ellis of acting especially thoughtful, he cared about his cousin. They had grown up as close as brothers. Thus, he made an effort. "You have never been eloquent," Ellis conceded. "Yet somehow, you are even less so today than usual. Perhaps you ought to begin again. You said you want to see Miss

Florence, yet you also seem to dread such a meeting. Given that she is your near neighbor, I cannot think catching sight of her is a rare thing. Why such opposing reactions to the idea on this particular day?"

Ellis kicked his feet up on a footstool and tucked his hands behind his head. He might as well settle in since Franklin lacked all ability to speak coherently at present.

"I hardly know where to begin." Franklin paced the room as he spoke, his long legs eating up the carpet in so few strides that the man couldn't possibly derive any satisfaction from the agitated march. "I have never taken much notice of her, until quite recently. Now, she is the only person I *wish* to notice. Do you understand?"

With a slow shake of his head, Ellis waited for his cousin to elaborate.

Franklin threw his hands upward, his fists exploding into an agitated, open-palmed gesture. "No one understands. Imagine this, if you will." Franklin pointed to the mantel. "Do you see that clock? What if you saw that clock every day? *Every single day* of your life, without realizing it was a clock. And then, finally, one day you walk into the room and the clock strikes the hour at the precise moment you wished to know the time. There. That must explain it."

"You are rubbish at metaphors." It took some effort not to laugh at the crestfallen expression on Franklin's face, but Ellis had pity on his friend and sat forward. "Say it plainly, man. You have taken notice of Miss Florence— but in what way?" Then he adjusted his cravat as he muttered, "She seems to have driven you to madness."

"Precisely so." Franklin visibly brightened, then the

poor fellow began quoting. "'Love is merely a madness,' as the bard says."

"I doubt Shakespeare—wait." Ellis bolted to his feet. "Did you say love? You think yourself in love with Miss Florence?" Ellis pointed at the clock. "Then what was all the ridiculous talk about clocks?"

His long, lean cousin dropped into the nearest chair with an impatient huff. "I was trying to explain how it came to be that I fell in love with her only recently, though I have known her all her life." Franklin glared at the clock. "Perhaps my metaphors need improvement."

"Or you could cease attempting them altogether." Ellis nudged the footstool out of his way and took up the pacing his cousin had left off. He wasn't as tall as Franklin, which meant his steps measured the distance from one end of the other perfectly. At least when it came to pacing. "You have never shown the slightest interest in Miss Florence before. Yet you now fancy yourself in love with her?"

"I *am* in love," Franklin insisted. He leaned back in his chair and threw his arm up over his eyes. "At least, I think I am. As I said, this is a recent development. Here we have been neighbors our whole lives, and yet I thought her no more than a child until that afternoon in the bookshop."

Ellis paused near the window, turning his back to it to stare at his cousin. "You fell in love with her...in a bookshop?"

"Are there better places to fall in love?"

"I have no objection to someone finding love amid books."

"Good. I had wondered. It seems ballrooms and gardens are more the thing. But it was raining, you see." A silly, sideways smile appeared on Franklin's face. "And we were both trapped in the shop by the sudden deluge. Then I saw what she had purchased and ventured to comment."

"Does what she purchased signify somehow?" Ellis asked, the conversation having left all definitions of sensible behind long before.

Franklin waved that question away. "No. Merely something for her sister. A book about Persia. I forget what it's called. The book itself isn't important." He sat up again, slapping his knees with his hands. "What matters is what followed. She is a creature of such refined tastes and elegance. She has grown from an adorable child into an angel-like woman. I have finally seen it for myself, and I am driven to distraction by the very thought of her."

"Driven to Bedlam, more like," Ellis said softly, shaking his head. "What have you done about it? Whom have you told?"

"Nothing and no one." Franklin dropped his head into his hands. "I haven't the faintest idea what to do."

Though Ellis cared deeply for his cousin, he knew well enough that Franklin had never been the steadiest of fellows when it came to his feelings. He was as like to flit from one pursuit or idea to another as a butterfly was to visit a daisy and then a daffodil. "I think you will have to do something that is quite impossible. Impossible for you, I mean."

"Such as?" Franklin peered up at Ellis from between his fingers.

"Say and do nothing to give away your feelings. At least—not until you are certain of them. As you say, you have never been in love before. What if you are mistaken?" Ellis folded his arms across his chest and fixed his cousin with a severe frown. "Imagine if you told the girl, or her parents, or anyone. And then, a week from today, you no longer felt the same? Perhaps the change in weather addled you. Or you mistake a passing fancy for true devotion. If you remain silent, and the feelings dissipate, you hurt no one." The alternative would likely cause a rift in the entire neighborhood.

Especially if Miss Jessica Nettle had anything to say about it. The woman had a vengeful nature, to be certain. Not that he thought her a villain, but rather an overly eager defender.

The other man's shoulders drooped. "So if I speak now, I could hurt Miss Florence? That is the very last thing I wish to happen, Ellis." His smile reappeared. "Which speaks in favor of my feelings for her, does it not?"

"It speaks in favor of your good nature." Ellis turned away from his cousin, focusing his stare out the window. "You wouldn't kick a dog if it meant to bite you."

"You are wiser than I in most things," Franklin admitted with a rueful lilt in his voice. "How will I know when to speak? When does one know if love is real and not a fanciful turn of the mind?"

A carriage emerged from the gray wood, where the path wound from the house to the road. His uncle and cousins returned from church. "Give it time, Frank. I am here through Epiphany. I will watch with you. We will see if your feelings are real and—better yet—if Miss Florence returns them."

And Saints help Franklin if he said or did anything that brought the wrath of the elder sister upon him.

A smile pulled at the corners of his mouth as he

considered what Jessica's reaction would be to learning her sister had an admirer. Perhaps she would finally have reason to turn her maddening attention away from Ellis and onto another poor soul for her tricks. Whatever came next, Ellis could only imagine this holiday season would be quite different from those of the past.

DEAR ESTHER

Brookfield House, Hatfield
December 16th, 1815

My Dearest Esther,

It is but seven days since my arrival at my nephew's house, and I already have found myself in the midst of a most amusing situation. Matters of the heart have never interested me—not since I found my own happiness in love. Yet I find my two great-nieces are both facing the prospect of youthful entanglements this very season. I had not ever thought to try my hand at matchmaking, but with the challenge issued, and *two* opportunities falling in my lap at once—I suppose I cannot help but try.

I shall give credit where it is due. My niece, Florence, came to me straight away to reveal the plot of her story and her sister's, thus far. I made no promises to the girl, except to say I would give her my honest opinion on matters. And so I shall.

My other niece, Jessica, is another story entirely.

While her younger, innocent sister is aflutter by the thought of playing a game of romance, Jessica is already embroiled in what could be the best of love stories. I dare not say more until I have studied the matter and organized my plans. Suffice it to say, while one child knows exactly what she wants, the other must fall a little deeper before someone points it out to her.

I do hope your holiday promises to be as diverting as my own.

Yours, Etc.,

Temperance

CHAPTER 3

THOUGH JESSICA DIDN'T CLAIM HERS TO BE A NATURALLY devious mind, she still had a knack for schemes. For *planning*, she should say. And the superior ability to note when people around her concocted their own enterprises. Shortly after Aunt Temperance's arrival, Jessica sensed something untoward going on between her younger sister and the matron.

They had spent a quarter of an hour alone, the day after Aunt Florence arrived. Since whatever had passed in that interview—which Jessica missed in order to assist her mother with the weekly dinner menu—the two conspirators had exchanged many knowing glances with one another. They had also contrived to meet again, and once when Jessica entered a room where only those two had been before, they had immediately stopped talking.

But it wasn't until after Church services that Jessica began unraveling their secret.

Jessica went to her sister's room to return the necklace she had borrowed—a very pretty strand of coral beads—

and found the door partway open. And her Aunt Temperance already inside, consoling a dispirited Florence, by the sound of things.

"...always there. I cannot think why he would not come today."

Aunt Temperance responded with her usual vivacity. "Perhaps he had a cold. Never mind. There will be plenty of opportunities for me to see the two of you together during my visit. Perhaps we can contrive to have him as a dinner guest this week?"

A happy gasp preceded Florence's answer. "Oh, that would be lovely. Then you could really get to know him."

Get to know whom? Jessica frowned at the crack, both upset with herself for eavesdropping and curious as to what more she might learn if she waited another moment to knock. Curiosity won out, as it so often did with her.

"While I am flattered that you hold my opinion so highly, I cannot help but wonder why you are keeping this from your sister. Surely, Jessica knows the gentleman well enough to have an opinion."

A thin, needle-like piece of ice stabbed Jessica's heart. Because Florence told Jessica everything. She always had. Yet here Florence spoke of a man. And why did women of her age speak of men, except as prospective husbands? But she hadn't mentioned any such person to Jessica. A person absent from church that very day.

Florence's answer to their aunt only hurt more. "Jessica's opinions about this gentleman are prejudiced. She has known him too long and thinks him foolish merely because of childhood games. I do not think she sees him as a man any more than she sees me as a woman grown." Her tone changed to one of impatience. "I will always be her infant sister, younger and in need of protection. No. Jessica cannot know about any of this until I have made up my mind."

The slippers Jessica wore made no sound on the corridor's carpet as she withdrew from her sister's room. She retreated all the way to the quiet of her mother's sitting room, which was empty for the moment. She stepped inside and closed the door behind her, lowering the latch with such care that it did not make its usual *click* when it caught.

Florence had a secret about a man. And she didn't intend for Jessica to know anything about that secret until it would be too late for Jessica to offer her advice or counsel.

"But," Jessica whispered to herself, "older sisters simply *must* protect younger ones." Everyone knew that. Jessica had never led her sister astray. If anything, the fact that Florence wanted to disguise her romantic interest from Jessica meant trouble. "Why would she not confide in me, unless she already has her own misgivings about the man?"

Though tempted to confront her sister about the issue, Jessica decided to bide her time. Proving to her sister that she could be both patient and circumspect. So when she walked to town with her sister the day after her eavesdropping, she pretended as though everything was as normal as always.

A chill in the air made Jessica shiver and tuck her gloved hands deeper into her muff. They passed Sainte Ethelreda's, a church built during the years of Norman conquest and now their place of Anglican worship. The old building stood out with almost black stone against the gray winter sky.

"How I let you convince me of a walk in this weather, I cannot understand," Jessica grumbled, though when Florence raised her eyebrows the elder sister had to smile.

Florence nudged her sister with her elbow, perhaps as unwilling as Jessica to remove her hands from her fur muff. "You were as eager as anything to walk to Boothe's to check on the progress of our ribbons."

"Perhaps." Jessica feigned a regretful sigh. "Though why I risk a pink nose and chapped lips for something as paltry as red and gold ribbon, I do not know." She had turned over in her mind how she might discover the man who held her sister's interest. Continuing the Christmas preparations seemed a likely enough way, given how often they must come in contact with neighbors during all the festivities.

The sisters entered Boothe's together. The shop boasted a beautiful array of ribbons and spools of thread, gold-tinted twine, bells and bobs, and every sort of bauble one might need to undertake a fabric-related project. Lengths of ribbon dangled from hooks above the windows, and elegant lace draped small tables in the corners. A tall counter ran the length of the shop, separating patrons from the keepers of thimbles and buttons.

Florence went directly to that divider, standing behind two matrons debating on silver or brass buttons. Jessica drifted to the window, examining the ribbons with half her attention while watching out the glass with the rest. The clouds above had darkened a few shades since they had left their home.

There was every chance they would return to Brook-field House damp if their business in town took too long. Of course, they could always step into the bakery. Mr. Thompson kept several tables and chairs for hungry patrons to sit and take tea. If they arrived there before the sky fell, they could wait out the rain.

A smudge of deep blue in her peripheral vision drew Jessica's attention away from the sky and to the street. A gentleman wore the color as a coat, and he stood before a display of boots in a shop across the road. She studied his familiar form, and the instant she realized why she recognized the broad shoulders and characteristic tilt of the head, he turned his head enough to reveal his profile, confirming his identity.

"Ellis Webb," she said softly, her warm breath fogging the window before her.

So. He had arrived. Perhaps the weather had delayed him. She knew the family had expected him on Friday or Saturday of last week. That she hadn't seen him in church had surprised her, but then—

A prickling dread clenched around her heart. The entire neighborhood had expected Ellis to appear in church on Sunday. But he hadn't been there.

The possibility that *he* was the man Florence had missed seeing at services made Jessica's heart pound against her chest most painfully. Florence couldn't harbor tender feelings toward Ellis! That prideful, arrogant, superior creature would break Florence's heart as soon as look at her. The man had no tact, no tenderness of feeling toward anyone but his cousin, and laughed far too freely at the missteps of others.

Jessica had spent years observing him and had half a

dozen situations she could use as proof of his inadequacy as a suitor. Of course, she had spent those same years doing her best to make him miserable. Because he deserved it.

Which would be precisely why Florence wouldn't want Jessica to know that she cherished the man. Admired him. Loved him? Oh, Jessica wouldn't bear that for even a moment. She couldn't. Her heart rebelled at the idea of so beloved a sister giving her affection to that... that...that horrid man!

"The ribbons will be delivered today," Florence exclaimed, her delighted words startling Jessica from her silent fuming.

"Oh. Wonderful. Yes." Jessica blinked back her fury. "Then we may adorn the house tomorrow."

"Just so." Florence peered out the window, causing Jessica to brace herself as she watched her sister. Surely, Florence would see Ellis. And her reaction would tell Jessica everything she needed to know. "Oh my. It looks as though the clouds will burst at any moment. Had we better go to the bakery?"

Jessica's gaze darted to the street. Ellis had disappeared. Her sister hadn't seen him.

"Yes. Of course. Before it rains."

Florence eyed Jessica with confusion. "Are you well, Jessica? You seem out of sorts. I hope it is not the rain that is causing you worry. You know that Father will send the coach if it rains more than half an hour. We needn't walk home in a deluge."

Forcing a smile, Jessica tried for a more natural speech. "You are right, of course. My mind was elsewhere.

It is only...I think you are right. I cannot give up the kissing ball tradition this year."

That brought a cheerful squeal from her sister, who immediately looped her arm through Jessica's and led the way out of Boothe's. "I knew you could not give it up so easily. We have always made mistletoe decorations, and we always will. It is part of the fun of the celebrations. Just like the Marquess of Salisbury's Twelfth Night ball."

The Marquess of Salisbury, as the chief resident of Hatfield, always threw a grand celebration at the end of the Christmas festivities. The sisters had attended since they came out into Society. But the pleasure of the event had diminished for Jessica with each passing year, as she watched friends and neighbors couple up at the event. Leaving her to the edges of the ballroom, watching as they made match after match.

The sisters entered Thompson's bakery, the bell above the door cheerfully announcing their presence. Florence led the way to a table near the window. They both sat, removing their muffs to let them rest in their laps. The bakery was warmed by the large ovens in the back, and it smelled of fresh bread, yeast, and spices that soothed Jessica's heart.

Cinnamon, cloves, and ginger mixed in the surrounding air. Mrs. Thompson appeared at their table. "What can I get you fine young ladies on this dreary day?" she asked pleasantly.

"Tea, please. And gingerbread biscuits," Florence declared.

"Do you have any of your honey cakes?" Jessica dared to ask. They were her favorite, and no one made the honey and almond cakes as delicious as the Thompsons.

They were just the right amount of sweet for Jessica, and the servings at the bakery were quite large and filling. Jessica could survive a whole day on a single slice.

"We do, dear. I will bring your tea and sweets directly." Mrs. Thompson went away. Six tables, small and round, were in the room. Only three, including theirs, were occupied. Few had ventured out under the threat of the weather, it seemed.

The sisters talked of ribbons while they waited, and the gifts they planned for their neighbors. Their family gave bundles of herbs to their closest friends every Christmas. They had fields and fields of fragrant herbs grown by their tenant farmers, sent to London and even farther afield. They also gave close friends wheels of cheese from their dairy cows. An exchange of such goods between the gentry had always been tradition in their community.

Rain pattered against the window as they discussed the merits of purchasing cakes from the bakery rather than weigh their own cook down with making treats for the children who lived nearby. Their poor cook would already be burdened with feeding the family and their callers, not to mention preparing a Christmas Eve feast for a dozen guests or more.

The bells above the bakery door jingled merrily as Mrs. Thompson set their teapot, cups, and plates of cake and biscuits before them. When the proprietress looked up to see her new customers, Jessica naturally did the same.

Ellis Webb and Franklin Thackery removed their hats, now dripping with the rain from outside. They were laughing with one another, removing their bulky wool overcoats to hang them on hooks near the door. And then

Ellis turned around, a smile still upon his face, and his gaze collided with Jessica's.

She hadn't seen him in a year. He had stopped visiting during the summer after leaving university. He only came for the Christmas celebrations, and Franklin went to wherever Ellis happened to be during the summer. Usually Scotland, or Cornwall, or some place interesting. A place far away.

Ellis appeared as handsome as ever. His chocolate-hued, damp hair fell in a wave over his forehead. His dark lashes framed his gray eyes, making the unique color stand out all the more. Though shorter than his cousin, Ellis had an air of confidence that had always made him seem like a knight stepped from the pages of a storybook. As a child, she had easily imagined him sparring with villains and saving lost princesses.

In the present, under her surprised scrutiny, he raised his eyebrows at her and tilted his head to the side. Asking her, quite plainly, why she stared.

Jessica tore her gaze from his and looked to her sister, whose back was to the door. Florence didn't know Ellis had entered the bakery. And now was the perfect time to see how she would react when she learned he was near.

When she spoke, her voice sounded far calmer than she felt. "It seems Mr. Webb has arrived for Christmas." There. That hadn't been difficult. Why had she ever thought it would be?

"Oh?" Florence put her cup down in its saucer. "Is Mr. Thackery with him?" she asked with a careful tone of voice. Did she pretend disinterest in Ellis?

Jessica lifted her teacup to hide behind its rim. "Yes, of course. They are coming this way."

Florence's posture stiffened, and her eyes grew wide. Her cheeks flushed. All evidence of more feeling than Jessica had ever seen from her sister when it came to gentlemen. Before she could make further study of her sister's reaction, the men stood at their table.

Franklin spoke to them. "Ah, Miss Nettle and Miss Florence. What a surprise to see you both today. Please, keep to your seats. We wouldn't dream of inconveniencing you, would we, Ellis?"

A half step behind his cousin, Ellis shook his head. "Not at all. Ladies. It is good to see you both." He darted a quick glance at his cousin. "In fact, as it has been so long since I have had the pleasure of speaking to you both, might we join you for refreshment?"

Jessica experienced several odd and conflicting emotions at once. Though she needed to observe her sister with Ellis to ascertain the depths of Florence's admiration, Jessica's heart felt that stab of ice again. Ellis and Florence were all wrong for one another. She knew it down to the depths of her soul, which had to explain how violently she rejected the idea of the two of them together.

Yet her polite answer slipped from her lips, as it must. "Please, do sit down, gentlemen."

She needed Ellis and Franklin to join them. But she also wished them on the other side of the county. Or the Continent.

Once the men had appropriated chairs from another table, they settled one between each sister. Mrs. Thompson appeared from the doorway to the kitchen with two cups, which she put down for the gentlemen before promising to return with their requested pastries.

All the while, Jessica watched her sister. Florence's cheeks bore a light blush, but otherwise, the girl appeared unflustered.

She kept her lashes lowered, too, and her fingers daintily clutching her teacup.

Jessica needed more to work from than her sister's shyness. Which was, she thought, somewhat uncharacteristic. Was this what love did to people?

Ellis broke the odd silence hanging around the table first. "It is a pleasure to see you both again after so long an absence from this part of the country." His lips curved upward on one side only, giving Jessica an idea his words were more sardonic than sincere.

"As you are so well traveled, Mr. Webb, I wonder at you coming back to our quiet town at all," she said, fluttering her lashes at him. "You never seem to settle anywhere for more than a fortnight." He would make a terrible match for Florence, who much preferred the comforts of home to even the idea of travel.

Not like Jessica, who longed to see more of the world than Hatfield and Hertfordshire.

"You make it sound distasteful to travel, Miss Nettle." His smile broadened, but also turned brittle. "For myself, I cannot understand why so many are content to stay in one place. Not when there is a wide world to see and discover."

"Oh, Jessica doesn't mind the idea of travel," Florence said, drawing Jessica's gaze to her. She tried by the widening of her eyes to discourage her sister from revealing such a thing, but Florence looked to Ellis instead of her sister. "She is forever studying tales of faraway lands. I think the speed of your travel is more what she remarks upon. Isn't that what you meant, Jessica?"

Rather than contradict her sister and risk a satisfied smirk from Ellis, Jessica nodded. "Yes. Quite." Then she adjusted her posture to look Ellis in the eye. "And you stole away our neighbor, Mr. Thackery, this summer last. You both went to Ireland, I believe."

Ellis grimaced and twisted in his chair—and she distinctly felt his booted foot brush her skirt on its way to kicking Franklin. She raised her eyebrows, and he feigned an innocent smile in her direction.

"We did," Franklin said, the words bursting from him with an incongruent desperation. His startled gaze darted from her, to Ellis, and then to Florence. "A beautiful island. You think England is green—you have never seen what Ireland gardens boast of. We went to the university in Dublin. A vast place. Most impressive."

"I understand their library is without equal," Florence said, turning her shy smile to Franklin. The pink in her cheeks turned darker. "Did you happen to venture inside?"

Franklin leaned toward her so slightly that Jessica wouldn't have seen it had she not been staring at him in some surprise. Now that the two had made eye contact, and Florence engaged him in talk of the library in Dublin, Jessica came to a new conclusion.

Ellis Webb did *not* hold her sister's romantic interests.

Her gaze darted to Ellis to find him watching Florence with interest as he sipped at his tea. He seemed perfectly aware of her preference, too. And happy to sit quietly while Franklin and Florence prattled on to each other about books chained to shelves and busts of famous philosophers.

Florence harbored a *tendre* for Franklin Thackery. Who also hadn't been at Sunday's worship services because he'd remained home to await the arrival of his cousin. But how had such feelings developed beneath Jessica's very nose without her noticing? When had Florence's feelings begun?

She narrowed her gaze at the oblivious couple, then turned pointedly to her right where Ellis sat quietly. He noticed her movement and lowered his teacup to give her a curious glance. For one blissful moment, relief ran through her veins as a warm comfort against the cold. Because Florence didn't want Ellis Webb. She wanted his cousin.

Still. That match was—while not as terrible—not altogether a good idea. She could immediately think of a dozen reasons the two of them couldn't possibly suit one another. Yet Ellis sat in seeming contentment, even with what appeared to be a full understanding of what took place in front of them.

Tipping her head a little his direction, Jessica spoke to him alone. "What are you looking forward to most during your visit, Mr. Webb?"

His eyes narrowed slightly. "I suppose the usual traditions of the year, Miss Nettle. Good company and food. Parties filled with amiable folk. Nothing out of the ordinary." His lips twisted in a knowing smirk. "Because nothing ever changes in Hatfield."

He enjoyed needling her about the smallness of her world. He always had remarked upon it, providing her yet another reason to antagonize him when the opportunity arose. And it would.

"Those of us who live here quite enjoy our traditions. They ensure we remain close to one another as a community, despite all outside influences." She made certain to sound appropriately repulsed by such influences and insinuate he was one of them with a well-measured glare.

Ellis's lips twitched. "And which traditions are your favorites, Miss Nettle?"

Florence broke away from her conversation with Franklin, more flushed than before. "Oh, Jessica loves nearly all of them. This is her favorite time of the year. She says so every December. I can only think on one aspect of our celebrations she has ever objected to, but even that—"

"—is of no consequence," Jessica said with false cheer before anyone could ask which tradition she had grown less and less enthusiastic about. She had no desire to open herself to further ridicule by Ellis. Especially since it was his fault she no longer saw the use of hiding mistletoe throughout homes during Christmas celebrations. She looked out the window to find the rain had stopped and let that discovery bring her to her feet. "Look, Florence. The rain has abated. I think we had better take advantage of the moment and return home before anyone worries about us."

The men rose, Franklin more slowly than Ellis, though he spoke first. "Yes, I suppose it would be best to go before it starts up again." He looked to Ellis, then to Jessica. "Would you like an escort on your return, Miss Nettle?" As the elder of the two sisters, it was her duty to approve or deny such a thing.

And as strongly as she wished to deny him, she could think of no polite way to do so. Through gritted teeth, Jessica agreed to the men accompanying them on the walk home. They had to retrieve their horses—the men had ridden into town together—but promised to meet the ladies on the old church road. As all four of them walked out of the bakery, Jessica composed a list within her thoughts. A list of all the reasons Franklin Thackery would never do as husband for Florence.

The one thing Jessica didn't know, however, was how to convince her sister to see things the same way.

CHAPTER 4

Two days after walking the Nettle sisters home from the bakery, Ellis had a headache. He blamed Franklin. The man wouldn't cease talking of Florence Nettle and all the perfection of her form, face, and thoughts. Though not usually in that order.

The only time Franklin's effusive praise abated was when other members of his family were in the room with them. As those other family members were young gentlemen with more energy than sense, sitting with them was equally dangerous to Ellis's health. If not more so.

Peter, aged sixteen, Benjamin, aged fourteen, and James, aged twelve, were rambunctious boys. Home from their schools for the winter holiday, they careened from one side of the house to the other in search of entertainment. The rain that had kept them indoors the past two days had turned to ice, not snow, which they consistently complained about.

Ellis escaped the drawing room they had taken over and slunk into the downstairs sitting room, where

Franklin found him. And immediately started waving a piece of paper in the air.

"Dinner," he said, his eyes as mournful as a calf's. "With the Nettle family. This very evening. What do you think of it, Ellis? Perhaps Miss Florence has persuaded her family to invite us."

It took some patience to settle his cousin's nerves and bring his expectations down from their lofty heights. "I am certain your neighbors often invite your family—your entire family—to dinner throughout the winter. Is not Mr. Nettle one of your father's dearest friends?"

"Oh." Franklin's shoulders fell, but the frenzied worry in his expression faded, too. The near-fever he had worked himself into regarding Florence Nettle had started to concern Ellis as much as it annoyed him. While he had been prepared to support his friend in a courtship, he wondered if Franklin was well enough equipped for a romantic venture. Usually, Franklin's nature of rushing head-long into adventure endeared him to his friends. But no one ought to rush into marriage.

"Steady on, Frank." Ellis gestured to a chair. "Sit. Think, if you will, how you might show the whole family that you are a worthy guest at their table. As you have *always* been." He sat across from his friend and resisted rubbing at his forehead to soothe the uncomfortable pain forming just behind his eyes. "You have little to prove. Just becalm yourself." *Please, for the sake of my sanity*, he silently added.

The idea of love had turned his cousin into a fool. If anyone could call what Franklin felt *love*. Perhaps what the man had truly attached himself to was the romance and not the woman. Surely, fancying a lady Franklin had known since infancy shouldn't drive him to such obsessive distraction.

Love ought to soothe a soul, not ignite it. At least, that's what Ellis saw in his own parents' union. Theirs was a steady affection, one of mutual respect. They conducted themselves with decorum, yet Ellis never doubted their feelings for one another. He had heard them confess to adoring one another often, from his childhood to adulthood.

Franklin possibly did not know what the characteristic signs of love were. Through no fault of his own, of course. Franklin's mother had passed away while the boy was young. His stepmother married his father when Franklin was already at school, then died after giving birth to her youngest son. He simply hadn't a ready example, and thus fate had left him unprepared to deal with members of the fairer sex.

Mr. Thackery, Franklin, Peter, and Ellis climbed into the family carriage at the designated hour. Peter sat with rigid posture, listening intently as his father drilled him again in good manners. It was the lad's first time invited to dinner with the adults. His younger brothers remained at home, not yet old enough for more formal occasions or the later hours.

Agitated by the moods of both sons, Mr. Thackery kept rehearsing to Peter all the mannerly things the boy had likely known since leaving the nursery. "And do not forget to cleanse your hands after eating. The water bowls Mrs. Nettle provides are more than adequate, and then you must dry your hands directly on the edge of the table-cloth if they have provided no napkins."

Ellis watched Franklin as his cousin agitatedly crumpled his dinner gloves, smoothed them out on his knees, then squeezed them into wads of white fabric yet again. One would think they were dining with the Crown Heads of Europe. Ellis refrained from comment and folded his arms tightly over his chest.

When they arrived at the house, Franklin stumbled all over himself in his greeting to his host and hostess. Mr. and Mrs. Nettle were cheerful and kind, as Ellis remembered. The couple led the four men into the drawing room adjacent to their formal dining room.

There, Mr. Nettle introduced them to his aunt. A woman of sixty, if she was a day, wearing an elegant purple gown edged in black lace. "It is a genuine pleasure to meet all of you," she said, her voice as elegant as her clothing. "Most especially the neighbors of my nephew. I have heard about the Thackerys of Lamblyn Court for years."

Franklin's chest puffed out as though she had declared him worthy of knighthood. The woman hadn't even really paid his family a compliment. She merely spoke of her curiosity. Her smile grew, and then she looked from Franklin to Ellis.

The top of Mrs. Bolingbrooke's head, when standing, didn't even reach Ellis's chin. But despite the gray at her temples and the wrinkles along her eyes and mouth, she had a vivacity to her when she spoke. And a twinkle in her eye that reminded him very much of Jessica Nettle, though he couldn't explain why.

"Mr. Webb. I am told you are often a guest in this house at Christmastide." Her head tilted the slightest degree, and Ellis had the strangest sensation of being measured. "Wherever do you go when you are not here?"

"Anywhere that sounds interesting," he admitted with a casual shrug. "My parents have a house in Bath, which means I often do my duty by visiting them there. But I prefer to travel rather than stay in one place."

"How interesting." Her gaze flicked from his head to the tips of his shoes. "I used to travel, too. Have you ever been as far as Cairo, in Egypt?"

Ellis had to fight to keep his composure, but he couldn't help the slightly eager note to his words when he said, "No, though it is my dearest hope to go there one day. Now that the war is over."

She nodded. "Good man. I highly recommend taking a barge down the Nile. It is good for a young person's constitution, I think. Going on such adventures." She nodded once again, then her gaze darted around his shoulder. "Ah, Jessica. There you are. I was just telling Mr. Webb he ought to make the trip to Egypt."

Stepping aside, Ellis opened their conversation circle to allow for Jessica to join them. She had entered the room without his notice. She stepped into the place between him and Franklin, and Ellis greeted her with a stiff bow.

Jessica had once come up behind him so quietly that he hadn't realized she was there until she dropped an icicle down the back of his collar. They had been at a small card party, the room full of conversation and laughter, but all had gone silent after Ellis released a bellow as the ice slid down his spine and caught itself at the waistband of his trousers.

Trying to pretend she hadn't assaulted him with ice and making unmanly excuses for his shout had ruined the evening for him. That had been two years ago.

The woman looked up at him now with wide, innocent eyes. But he saw the tiny lift to her lips, the spark of mischief in her eyes, and he knew—he knew she was thinking of that same childish prank. "Mr. Webb," she said with one slow blink, "do you plan to take a trip in crocodile-infested waters in the near future?"

He feared large reptiles less than he did Jessica Nettle.

He looked down at her comfortably, without having to strain his neck much. The eldest Nettle daughter was the tallest of her sisters, making her nearly eye-level with him. "I have no thought of Egypt at present, Miss Nettle. Though I plan to see Rome in the spring."

For an unaccountable reason, her face paled. Her lips parted slightly, too. The emotion, whatever it was, lasted only a moment before she was smiling again. "How wonderful for you. I am certain the ancient city must be beautiful in the spring." She swallowed tightly, then looked pointedly to the other side of the room.

Only then did Ellis realize Franklin had left the conversation to hover at Miss Florence's elbow. She stood by a pianoforte, looking through sheets of music, and he leaned in close. But he wasn't looking at the music. He was staring up at her, his gaze unwavering.

Ellis barely refrained from groaning aloud. His cousin had absolutely no subtlety to him.

Mrs. Bolingbrooke had followed his gaze across the room. "Aren't they an elegant couple?"

Her question startled him. Ellis looked to the matron, who opened a feathered fan with a languid gesture. "But then, I suppose any two young people of good breeding would look lovely together, don't you?" She held him with her stare, waiting for his answer, a challenge in her eyes.

Who *was* this old woman, and why did he feel the need to raise his defenses beneath her fierce inspection?

Most unexpectedly, Jessica allied herself with him. "Quite right. Just as any two peacocks would look lovely upon the lawn." Suddenly, Jessica's arm was on his. "I think it is time to go in to dinner. The senior Mr. Thackery will escort you, Aunt Temperance."

The elderly woman raised her eyebrows at her niece but floated away from them both toward Ellis's uncle. Ellis looked down to where Jessica's gloved hand rested at the crook of his arm. Then he met her gaze with a raised eyebrow.

She narrowed her eyes at him. "Is something troubling you, Mr. Webb?"

"Only the knowledge that the last time you touched my arm, you managed to leave behind a spider." Last year. That particular prank had happened on his last day visiting Franklin. The spider hadn't been real, of course. Merely a small ball of string artfully arranged to look like the body and appendages of an eight-legged fiend.

That had been outside of church, after the service marking Epiphany. Ellis hadn't seen the spider until after Franklin yelped and struck his arm, trying to kill the creature but only bruising Ellis. He had picked up the brown-threaded spider from the snow and had to bite the insides of his cheeks to keep from laughing. He'd looked up to see Jessica across the churchyard, hands tucked innocently in her muff, watching him with a wide grin.

He'd thought, for one confusing moment, that he rather liked her grinning at him that way.

"I have a proposal for you." Her words broke through his musings, and he smirked.

"Usually, it's the gentleman who says those words to the lady. But perhaps you were not aware of that convention."

Jessica wrinkled her nose at him. "Do be sensible."

"I am not the one always playing childish games, Miss Nettle." He pushed his shoulders back and wiped the smile from his face. "I have always been the more sensible of the two of us."

The doors to the dining room opened, and the couples lined up, Franklin and Miss Florence directly behind Ellis and Jessica. Jessica glowered at him, then hurriedly whispered, "Very well. I will keep my thoughts on the matter of your cousin and my sister to myself." She tipped her nose into the air, and he said nothing more until after he'd helped her into her chair and settled into his. Directly next to Jessica.

Across the table from them, Franklin and Miss Florence sat together. She, appearing lovely as an angel, Franklin, looking as eager as a puppy desperate for even a morsel of attention. The poor fool.

This really couldn't go on.

On the pretense of serving Jessica from a bowl of potatoes, Ellis leaned closer to her. "About that proposal..."

"Reconsidering your options, are you?" she asked, both eyebrows arched. She lifted her fork. "And I thought you'd chosen a gentlemanly spinsterhood."

He nearly dropped the potato onto the ivory tablecloth. "I mean my cousin—"

She smirked, and Ellis had his revenge by dropping the potato in the very center of her plate, where it came in contact with a small pile of peas, sending them rolling into the rest of her food.

"Perhaps I ought to serve myself."

"I wouldn't dream of inconveniencing you, Miss Nettle."

They had been speaking under cover of the conversations flowing around them. On his right sat Peter, who was attempting to speak with the eldest Nettle son across the table. On her left was his father, engaged in a conversation across the table with Mrs. Bolingbrooke.

She stripped off her gloves, glaring at him as each finger slipped free of the satiny cloth. She laid them upon her lap, then lifted her fork. He thought she meant to ignore him completely, but then she whispered from the side of her mouth. "My aunt is playing at matchmaking."

Ellis tilted his head, watching her from the corner of his eye. "Franklin and Miss Florence?"

She glowered at her plate. "Yes. For an entire week. Since she arrived."

That could explain Franklin's sudden interest in Miss Florence. If someone had interfered, perhaps guiding the two young people together, Franklin's head might easily turn.

"Did your aunt happen to send your sister to the bookshop since her arrival?" he asked, thinking of the moment Franklin had described to him.

"Yes." Jessica lowered her fork to the plate. "Why?"

"Hm." Perhaps Franklin wasn't as besotted as he thought. All his feelings might well result from the elder woman's meddling. His exasperating infatuation was more likely to have an untimely end if it had been artificial from the start. "What was it you wished to speak to me about? Regarding the matter at hand?"

Jessica's lips curled slowly upward, and her lashes

lowered prettily. Before she could answer, her aunt spoke across the table.

"What conversation do those young people have, I wonder, that prohibits them from noting there are others in the room?"

Jessica's cheeks reddened, and Ellis immediately stiffened in his chair.

"They are probably threatening one another," Franklin said with a jovial grin.

Ellis wanted to kick him under the table, as he had done at the bakery. "Not so, I assure you."

"Threatening one another?" Mrs. Bolingbrooke snatched upon those words with troublesome quickness. "Dear me. I thought they were childhood friends, given that all of you spent the holidays running about the same neighborhood."

"Not so, Aunt Temperance." That was Mr. Nettle from the head of the table, hiding a grin behind his napkin. "I am afraid these two cross swords regularly. I used to have conversations with Jessica about her silliness. But I think they are both too grown to engage in their battles anymore."

Ellis heard Franklin mutter, "Unlikely."

When Jessica's smile turned brittle, Ellis had to stop himself from leaning away from her. When she spoke, it was with an absolute air of innocence. "Of course, Papa. I am far too old for such antics."

Ellis didn't believe her. At all.

~

Jessica watched her sister and Franklin throughout the meal. Her sister barely said a word, but the gentleman stumbled about in his speech most awkwardly. Occasionally, Aunt Tempie would intervene in their clumsy attempt at conversation and give both young people enough confidence for them to smile.

The scene appeared like a poorly acted play. Without Aunt Tempie's support, the two never would get anywhere.

Which was why their match could never be. If they had not enough affection to even make simple conversation at dinner, they had no business flirting with one another. Which took Jessica back to her original purpose in speaking to Ellis.

Ellis, who apparently hadn't forgotten a single one of her small retributions against him. The satisfaction that knowledge gave settled warmly in her chest. Over the years, he had put up with her antics without once acknowledging them outside of a pointed glare. He had never asked what he had done to merit her ire, either.

The women rose from the table. Mrs. Nettle, Aunt Tempie, Florence, and Jessica, and returned to the drawing room. Florence went directly to the pianoforte to shuffle through her music again, a secretive smile playing on her lips.

Aunt Tempie took up a position near the instrument while Jessica's mother called for a servant to arrange for tea. Jessica wavered near the doorway, uncertain where to sit. Until Aunt Tempie raised her graying eyebrows and patted the empty place on the settee beside her. Florence had already started playing a lovely piece by one of her favored Austrian composers.

After Jessica had settled into the seat, Aunt Tempie leaned toward her. "What is all this I hear about you and Mr. Webb? Mr. Franklin Thackery and Florence have mentioned it now. Are the two of you sworn enemies?"

Others had asked this before. Jessica had no difficulty with her answer. "Not at all. We are quite civil with one another, as I am sure you saw at dinner."

"Do you both engage in battle, my dear, or is your war quite one sided?"

Jessica raised her eyebrows. "As I said, we are civil—"

"England has had a civil war before, my dear." Aunt Tempie used her fan to tap Jessica on the wrist. "You cannot dismiss my line of questioning. Does Mr. Webb return your fire volley for volley, or is he in an impenetrable stronghold, calmly waiting for you to withdraw your troops?"

The warlike imagery her aunt conjured with her words made Jessica pause in her answer. Put that way, her mild pranks sounded a great deal more intrusive. And Ellis had returned none of her pranks in years, making him the stoic stronghold and she the ineffectual militant. A most unflattering picture.

Yet one thing kept her from feeling too ridiculous. "He fired the first shot, Aunt Tempie." Jessica pretended to adjust the fingers of her gloves to avoid her aunt's probing stare. "That must count for something."

It counted for everything to her. Even if Ellis had forgotten the moment he humiliated her. The moment she couldn't forgive him for, because it still smote her heart with the same pain it had when she was fifteen years old.

Aunt Tempie pursed her lips, her brow wrinkled.

"Declared war, did he? I suppose it justifies things. A little." She flicked open her feathery fan. "Still. One would think you might call an occasional truce. It is nearly Christmas, and the days preceding Epiphany are meant to be peaceful and reflective."

Jessica turned that idea over in her mind. A truce. Not a terrible idea. Though she did not think her aunt meant for her mind to take that thought a wholly different direction. A cease-fire with Ellis might help matters with Florence and Franklin.

She meant to propose that Ellis keep Franklin far away from her sister, just so long as Aunt Tempie remained visiting. A determined matchmaker as clever as her aunt might put any two souls together with success, but whether they stayed together happily would be a different matter. Her thought had been simply to keep them apart. But if they had already sown the seeds of affection, that wouldn't be enough.

A new plan had grown in her mind by the time the drawing room doors opened and the men returned to the ladies' company.

Franklin went immediately to stand beside the pianoforte.

Jessica rose from her seat and drifted to the window on the other side of the room from the instrument. She noted Mr. Thackery took her vacated seat with a broad smile for Aunt Tempie, which meant her aunt would be occupied in conversation. Perfect. She wouldn't take much notice of Jessica enacting the first steps of her plan to spare her sister a foolish match.

Before she could fully form a plan to speak to Ellis alone, his reflection appeared beside hers at the window.

Dark as it was outside, the view hadn't brought him there. He stood behind her, close enough for her to feel the warmth of him at her shoulder.

"Miss Nettle."

She watched his reflection in the darkened glass. "Mr. Webb."

His reflection's lips went up on one side. "I believe there was something about which you wished to speak to me."

Why did her throat tighten and her heart race? After all this time, did she still have to fight away those childish feelings about him? Perhaps a truce was a terrible idea. Plotting subtle revenge against him was easier. Practicing offensive tactics had to be better for her heart than the defenses she would be required to employ if she raised a white flag now.

Her reflection in the glass appeared uncertain. Which would never do. Jessica tilted her chin up, daring herself to back down. "I did, in fact." She turned her back on the night outside the window and met Ellis's steady gaze. "I wish to call a truce."

That didn't cause the unflappable gentlemen to so much as wince. "A truce. Between the two of us?"

"Yes."

"As I have done little to progress the antagonism between you and me, I fail to understand the point of a truce. Surely, that would mean both sides are equally engaged in battle."

Though she railed against it, a blush warmed her cheeks. A one-sided battle made her efforts to that point feel small and immature. Best to pretend she didn't care.

Which meant squaring her shoulder and shuttering her expression imperiously. "A cease-fire on my side, then."

His gaze held hers a moment, then darted over her shoulder to the window behind her. "I assume you have a reason for proposing what must seem to you to be a retreat."

All the battle talk wearied her, which made her tone rather impatient. "I do have reason. My aunt's match-making is ridiculous. We both know that Florence and Franklin—Mr. Thackery—are ill-suited to one another. As his closest confidant, you must agree with me."

He met her eyes again, this time with a tilt to his head and a new angle to his smile. "I can agree that my cousin knows nothing about love. Therefore, he might mistake a temporary interest for undying affection."

"Which would be disastrous for my sister's heart." She glimpsed over his shoulder to where the two people they spoke of were staring at one another while her sister's fingers flew across the pianoforte's ivory keys. "And make for many a painful moment afterward, given our proximity as neighbors."

"Yes, I imagine that would be uncomfortable." Ellis smoothed his cravat, drawing her attention to the ruby stickpin within it. She stilled, staring at the gem that she hadn't taken the time to notice before.

A red stone, set in the jaws of a silver lion.

Her heart picked up speed, and a dull rush of blood filled her ears. The last time she had seen that cravat pin had been the night he received it as a gift from his parents. At the Christmas party her family held every year. At fifteen, she hadn't been out in Society yet. But her parents had allowed her to attend the family event.

She and Ellis, four years her senior, had been friends. He'd not visited that summer—the first time that had been the case—because he had wanted to travel before starting University. She'd missed him terribly and realized, as she'd longed for his company, that she felt more for the boy than friendship.

Jessica pushed away the memories before they overwhelmed her with regret. She clenched her gloved hands into fists and looked fixedly into his eyes. "If the two of us work together, perhaps we can prevent our relatives from ending their infatuation in tragedy. That is what I propose. Think on it, won't you? I plan to ride tomorrow at two o'clock. You can find me then, if you agree."

She skirted around him and walked with firm steps to the other side of the room to sit between her parents on the couch, happy to take what comfort she could from being near them.

Despite her attempt to ignore the rising memory, it came to her anyway. She clenched her hands together in her lap and directed her eyes to the fire. That wretched pin. Why did he still wear it?

The ruby in the lion's mouth had winked at her that Christmas past. She had spent the fortnight leading up to Christmas studying Ellis, her girlish heart entirely his for the taking. He had treated her as he always did every time he and Franklin were in her company. As a friend. Another child of the neighborhood he adopted every holiday. Meanwhile, her adoration of him increased as she noted everything from the handsomeness of his smile to the deep tones of his laugh.

On Christmas Day, she'd found him at her family's party and stayed near his side. She had hidden a kissing ball amid the greenery decorating the house, and with careful maneuvering, had placed the two of them beneath it. Then she had waited, likely turning blue from holding her breath, for him or someone—anyone—to notice they stood beneath the mistletoe-filled kissing ball.

Franklin had approached, and she'd met his gaze before pointedly looking upward. He'd followed her gaze and grinned. Then, still several paces away from his cousin, he'd said loudly, "You better run, Ellis. Jessica's caught you under the kissing ball."

Oh, how she'd blushed. But then she'd turned to Ellis hopefully, tilting her head slightly upward. Making it easy for him to fulfill the holiday obligation of a kiss beneath the mistletoe.

Ellis had looked up. Smirked. Then laughed. He'd met her earnest gaze, and the laugh had momentarily faded. Then he'd shaken his head. "I cannot possibly kiss Jess. She's only a child."

Her heart shattered, she had taken a step away from him. Had feigned a smile while a forced giggle stuck in her throat. Another step back. The mistletoe hung over him alone. Of course. Ridiculous of her to think—

"I suppose not," Franklin had said, laughing at the idea himself. "Come, Ellis. They've set up the cards in the other room."

"I'll be right there." Ellis had watched his cousin walk away. Then he'd studied Jessica, and his smile had faltered. She had quickly lowered her gaze to his cravat, to the ruby in the lion's jaw. Unable to look him in the eye even a moment longer, lest he see how his words had hurt her. "A charming prank, Jess. But it will never work." He winked at her. "Perhaps try another tactic, then." And he'd walked away, leaving her alone and humiliated. Relegating her feelings into the realm of childish tricks.

The splintered pieces of her heart had pained her for some time to come, until she'd taken hold of his words. Another tactic? Another prank, he meant. Very well. If all he expected from her was mischief and larks, that's what she would give him.

And so she had. Every time he visited. Until this truce.

In the present moment, her mother leaned close to whisper in Jessica's ear. "Are you all right, darling?"

Jessica blinked away the past and reassured her mother with a smile. "I am well. Merely thinking of our Christmas plans."

"Lovely, darling. I think this will be our best celebration yet." Her mother's gaze drifted to Florence and Franklin across the room.

Jessica's gaze went a different direction, to Ellis standing at the window still. He stared at his cousin with a contemplative expression. "Yes, Mama. I believe it will."

CHAPTER 5

FOG UNFURLED FROM ELLIS'S LUNGS. HE SAT ATOP HIS borrowed mount, back straight as a soldier's, watching his warm breath puff out into the cold air. When Jessica had suggested riding, she could not have known how abominably cold it would turn all at once. He knew there were places in England already covered in the white of snow and ice, but he'd hoped to avoid freezing to death in Hertfordshire.

He waited in a stand of trees with a fine view of Brookfield's stable yard. If she left the stable, mounted, he would see her. Then he could intercept her on the road or in the field.

Perhaps Jessica never intended to meet him. She'd dangled the lure of a truce, knowing he would take the bait, and then remained warm and snug by her fire at home. Laughing at him.

It wouldn't be the first time she had outmaneuvered him with a jest. But she had seemed in earnest this time. Her objection to her sister and his cousin forming an attachment had appeared genuine. Her reasoning was sound, insofar as she had explained it.

The horse snorted a cloud of white and stamped its foreleg with impatience. Ellis well understood the animal's discomfort, and he leaned forward to soothe the horse with his touch. "There we are, my good fellow. Not much longer. A gentleman must give a lady the benefit of the doubt, you see." He checked his pocket watch, his gloved fingers making it difficult to open the silver face. "We leave at a quarter past two."

Why had the temptation of a truce proven too much for him? For nearly seven years, he'd tolerated Jessica's pranks and witticisms. She had performed nothing truly malicious, of course. And interspersed with her mischief, he had still caught glimpses of a sweet nature. The kindly, soft part of herself that she shared with everyone—everyone except him.

"It wasn't always like this," he remarked aloud to the horse. One brown ear flicked back to him, which he took as an invitation to continue his musings. "She was a kind child. There weren't too many years separating us, you see. When we visited, she would follow Frank and me about. I was genuinely fond of her."

He still was, if he were honest with himself. If Jessica had any inkling of that fondness, he'd no doubt she'd be utterly shocked. Perhaps even scandalized by the knowledge that her enemy found her intriguing rather than infuriating. He guarded that secret, even from Franklin.

He had never pinpointed when things had changed between them. One day she had eagerly asked after his adventures, and another he'd found raw eggs in the bottom of his boot. With his stockinged foot. That had been unpleasant and had bewildered him for two full days before he'd realized Jessica had something to do with it.

Around that same time, she'd stopped calling him Ellis, and he'd begun to refer to her as Miss Nettle. At least, when he spoke of her to others. She was still Jessica in his mind. Even if the fair-haired girl in white dresses with pink ribbons had grown. Grown right up into womanhood, wearing sly smiles and jewels in her ears and at her throat.

Ellis smiled to himself, picturing the woman in his mind as she had glared at him the evening before.

When her blue eyes sparked with irritation, the green rings at the center seemed to grow more pronounced. Dragon-like, he imagined. Warning all in her path of her ire. And last night, her ire hadn't been directed toward him. For once. She had been too focused on Franklin and Miss Florence.

The horse stomped again, and Ellis focused on the scene before him one last time. He'd been lost in his thoughts and had missed Jessica's exit from the stable. She rode a striking black horse, its legs striped in white. And they came directly toward where he waited, tucked back in the trees. As the horse cantered across the frozen ground, Ellis had eyes only for the rider.

She wore a red riding habit with a pointed cap adorned in long pheasant feathers. And she didn't seem to see him until she had come halfway across the field to the tree line. He saw the way her posture changed, lapsing for a moment from the fluidity of a practiced rider into something stiff. But she didn't slow her approach.

Not until they were near enough to speak.

A dark blue scarf wound its way around her shoulders and neck. She pulled it down away from her mouth with an impatient tug. "Mr. Webb." She raised her honey-blonde eyebrows upward. "I wasn't sure whether to expect you."

"And yet here I am," he said, making a show of withdrawing his watch. He popped the front open and casually observed the time. "And you, my dear Miss Nettle, are twelve minutes late."

She batted her lashes at him. "How terribly rude."

"Yes, but I forgive you."

"I didn't ask for your forgiveness."

Ellis blinked. "But you said—"

"I accused you of rudeness," she announced with a disdainful sniff. "You never ought to tell a lady she is late. Or hasn't your mother taught you that?"

Ellis narrowed his eyes at her. "I beg your pardon—"

"Then you are forgiven," she said airily, as though she hadn't cut off his speech. She guided her horse down the path, her back to him.

"That isn't what I meant," he muttered. But he wanted a truce with her. Even if she meant to make it difficult on him. Because Jessica wasn't all prickles, and it was high time for the two of them to get along again.

With no choice but to follow her, Ellis wheeled his horse around and caught up to Jessica. The path was just wide enough for the two of them to ride shoulder-to-shoulder, but he let her have the lead by a foot.

Perhaps bringing her to the point speedily would be the best course of action. "Yestereve, you said something about a truce."

Her voice floated back to him. "I did." Then she said

nothing.

He counted to twenty in his head before giving in to whatever game she wished to play by making him ask. Most women, he felt he understood. But Jessica always left him wondering what went on within her clever mind.

"Are we going to speak of your plan?" he asked, raising his voice for it to carry ahead of him. "Or am I to follow along blindly?" Not that he minded the view. His gaze trailed down from the loose curls at her neck to the tightly cinched waist of her riding coat. Despite the added bulk of the garment, he made out her slender form readily enough. The woman likely turned heads wherever she went, as fair of figure and face as she was.

Why wasn't Franklin enamored with *this* sister? Florence was a lovely girl, but Jessica had something entirely her own about her. She wasn't going to wilt at the first sign of trouble. He imagined quite easily a woman of her character as at home on the back of a camel as she was on her fine thoroughbred.

"I suppose it is time we discuss things." She directed her horse to the side and stopped, waiting for him to come abreast with her. Ellis sighed but followed through. When their horses stood side-by-side, she turned her head to look him over. "The terms of the arrangement are simple. I will suppress my desire to have a laugh at your expense, and you will help me keep Mr. Franklin Thackery and my sister from forming any serious attachment."

"That doesn't sound simple at all." And Ellis wasn't about to let her make all the rules. "I have to know a few things and get some reassurances from you. For one thing, I will not have Frank harmed merely because he admires your sister without your approval. For another, what the devil does 'suppress' your desire mean? It sounds as though you might still try to get away with your usual waggery."

She placed a hand over her chest and affected a most innocent, wide-eyed expression. "You question my word, sir? Will you not trust me?"

He smirked, unable to hide his amusement. Though he would happily do without her pretty jokes, he never minded their verbal sparring. "Until the end of time, Miss Nettle." He purposefully clarified nothing in that statement.

For some reason, that brought a pretty rose blush into her cheeks. She cleared her throat, then nodded once. "Very well. I suppose we could have more detailed rules and plans. If that sets your mind at ease."

"It does." He nudged his horse forward on the riding trail, taking a turn at leading them both. "When you explained your objections to a match between Frank and your sister, you said you wished to help her avoid any pain that a false affection would bring. And the awkwardness in the neighborhood after the fact, too. Is that accurate?"

"Yes. I suppose." She did not sound wholly convinced of her own reasons.

Ellis sighed. "While I have to admit to suffering great annoyance with my cousin over this past week, I cannot dismiss his feelings entirely. He thinks his affection for your sister is the beginnings of something greater."

She made as though to scoff at the idea, but Ellis cut her a sharp, sideways glance, keeping her from speaking. "I imagine, for you to be as concerned as you are, that your sister has made similar statements. At the very least, she has hinted at such an attachment."

"Yes." She narrowed her eyes at him. Then she shifted her gaze away. "With Aunt Temperance employed to help with the matchmaking. I think my sister is the catalyst of this whole nonsense."

"And yet"—he held one gloved finger in the air to make his point—"what if it is not nonsense? What if they truly care for one another? Would you, Miss Nettle, separate your sister from a man she adores?"

The woman's forehead wrinkled, and she averted her gaze from his. "I would never want that. But this cannot possibly be love. Florence is too young. And Frank—Mr. Thackery has been our neighbor our whole lives. If it was love, then why now? Why not sometime before? I think it is only my aunt's meddling that has driven them both to a frenzy."

"A frenzy?" Ellis chuckled, thoroughly amused. "That is over-stating the situation, surely."

Her lips twitched up, but she hastily put her superior mask back in place. "Perhaps."

"Here is what I propose." Ellis faced forward again, resisting the temptation to watch her as he spoke. "Rather than the two of us align ourselves to end Frank and Miss Florence's budding romance, we come together with a different goal first. I suggest we set ourselves to testing their bond of affection. If it proves true—"

"If they love each other, you mean," she stated bluntly, forcing him to look her direction. She regarded him with thinly veiled amusement. "You can say that word, Mr. Webb. It isn't as terrible as some oaths I've heard men utter."

Ellis hadn't any idea he had avoided the word until that moment. "Fine." He narrowed his eyes at her. "If we find proof that they are in *love*, we leave them alone and allow nature to take its course."

"See?" She grinned at him, and his heart skipped most irrationally. "That word isn't so difficult to say, is it?"

Still alarmed by the sudden activity within his chest, Ellis spoke more sharply than he intended. "Never mind that. Do you agree to let them alone if they are truly in love?"

Her smile faded, and she turned from him to stare ahead at the trail once again. "Of course. I would never stand between my sister and her happiness."

"Good." Ellis cleared his throat. "Excellent." He had to bite his tongue to keep from rambling, which meant they rode in silence for an uncomfortable stretch of time. The only sounds were the swaying of bare branches in the wood, and the hooves of their horses on the hard-packed earth.

He ought to apologize for his tone. No gentleman should snap at a woman like that. Even if his own organs had turned against him at the sight of a single dazzling smile. A smile that he had seen much more frequently before the woman at his side decided to despise him.

Again, the nagging question came into his thoughts. What had he done to merit her ire? If he asked at that very moment, might she tell him?

A shivering breeze came through the trees and across their path, making them both shudder. Ellis looked upward at the heavy gray clouds. "I think the sky means to drop on us. Perhaps snow."

"The mercury had dropped to freezing before I left for our ride." She looked upward, too.

"The mercury?"

"I keep a thermometer in my window." She shrugged one shoulder, not quite meeting his eyes.

An interesting idea. Instead of a perfectly acceptable comment, he blurted, "Why?" At least he sounded curious rather than rude. This time.

Jessica regarded him somberly for a moment, as though to ascertain his reasons for asking. Then she looked away, affecting a careless tone. "Living in Hertford-shire isn't as exciting as travel, of course, but I content myself with that by making observations of nature. Weather patterns. The change of seasons. It is a way to make the ordinary more interesting."

Ellis recognized an olive branch when Jessica extended it. She offered him a glimpse into her true self. He relaxed. They were back on even footing.

"There has been a thin layer of ice on the skating pond every morning, too." Her horse snorted, drawing her attention away from him to give the animal a soothing pat along its neck.

"I will help you determine if my cousin and your sister are truly in love." He adjusted the reins in his gloved hands. "But if we determine they are not—if it is only the meddling of a matchmaker at work—we will do our best to bring them to their senses by whatever means you deem necessary."

"Thank you." She stopped her horse, and he did the same. "Truly, Mr. Webb. Thank you."

It was on the tip of his tongue, to ask her to call him Ellis again. As she had when they were younger. But then the first snowflake fell between them, and then another landed on her red coat. And another. And another.

Ellis looked upward, then raised both eyebrows at her.

"Snow."

"At last." She smiled again, up at the sky rather than at him. Yet his vexatious heart twisted again, and Ellis had to hold his breath to steady it. She turned her horse about. "I had better return home."

The snowflakes were falling at a steady speed already. This was no slow-start to winter. "Do you know what today is?" he asked before she could leave.

She blinked at him. "Thursday. December the twenty-first."

He grinned at her. "The first day of winter."

"Are you a druid, Mr. Webb?" she asked, raising her eyebrows. "Good Christians don't celebrate the Winter Solstice, you know."

He grinned at her. "And yet, we make merry at Christmas tide with the same dedication our druid ancestors must have met the season with. And did you know that the old stone circles of England still align with the seasons? As do the ancient structures of the old world—from Egypt to India." Why had he started this conversation with her? He'd had some idea of imploring her to stay longer, perhaps.

But her smile diminished to something almost sad. "I will have to take your word for it, sir. I doubt I will ever see such things. Good day to you, Mr. Webb." Then she nudged her horse down the path, away from him and back to her home.

Ellis watched her go and wondered at the way he yearned to go after her.

Perhaps the time had come to make a concentrated effort, on his part, to return into Jessica Nettle's good graces.

CHAPTER 6

THE SNOWFALL HADN'T ABATED AFTER AN HOUR OR EVEN A day. It continued falling through the next evening, sometimes light as a feather and others in thick sheets of lace. Jessica watched from the window of her mother's sitting room, a deep blue shawl wrapped tightly around her shoulders. Behind her, her aunt and mother sat on the sofa with a table pulled near them for their work threading boughs of greenery with holly berries and ribbons.

Florence sat in a chair with her own little table, putting the finishing touches on a mistletoe-laden kissing ball. She had tried to convince Jessica to do more than wrap a sprig of mistletoe in gold ribbon, but Jessica had not allowed her sister to sway her. Thus her little clutch of mistletoe with its white berries rested innocently on the mantel until Jessica could bother to find some place to hide it. Or cast it into the hearth when no one was looking.

"Jessica, come away from that window," her mother

called, and Jessica turned to see the concern on her face. "Sit by the fire where it is warm. That glass is far too thin to keep the cold from you. I cannot have you falling ill before our Christmas party."

"Because you mean to use me as a skilled laborer," Jessica teased, though she obeyed and drew nearer to the fire and the other women. "I cannot help it. Falling snow is one of the most beautiful things in creation." She stood over her sister's shoulder, watching as Florence stitched green ribbons together.

"I quite agree," the younger woman said, smiling secretly to herself. Likely planning where she would hide her bit of decoration and how she would lure Franklin Thackery to stand beneath it.

Jessica's throat tightened, and she stepped away, thinking of the kiss she had yearned for and never received. Truly, quite ridiculous of her to still be affected by a childhood fancy.

"Dear me." Mother rose, brushing her skirt free of bits of thread. "Look at the hour. I promised your father we would discuss our schedule for Christmas. I will return in half an hour, ladies. Do continue without me."

"Yes, Mama," Florence said with a knowing glance at Jessica.

Mutton, the white-haired terrier, lifted his head from the rug to watch their mother leave. Then he yawned, his jaw gaping open widely, before snapping his mouth shut and rolling over on his back, keeping his belly toward the fire. The sisters giggled at him.

After their mother had shut the door behind her, leaving the warmth in the room with them rather than the cool corridor, Florence sighed happily. "I am quite sure there is nothing so wonderful as a lasting love."

Their mother would take longer than the promised time. Once she and their father bent their heads over any task, they found they enjoyed being in one another's company too much to part again easily. Theirs was a love match, and the years hadn't dimmed the ardor they felt for one another.

Jessica had to bite her tongue. She wandered over to the couch to take her mother's place next to Aunt Tempie. "Perhaps adventure might be as wholly encompassing. What do you think, Aunt?"

"You will not find me touting one over the other," Aunt Tempie said without looking up from her work. "I have known both, and they have so interwoven together that I could not possibly separate the two."

"You talk about your adventures all the time," Jessica said, sounding almost reproachful. "But never your romance."

Aunt Tempie's hands paused, and she looked over the rims of her spectacles at Florence first and then Jessica. "And just who do you think accompanied me on all my adventures? Your great-uncle, of course. Thomas was with me through thick and thin." She directed her gaze to the window, and her wrinkles deepened with her smile. "You know, it was during a snowstorm that I first met my Thomas."

The sisters looked at one another, then Jessica leaned closer to her great-aunt. "You never told us that. Or anything about how you met."

"You have never asked, Jessica. You have always been more interested in tales of ancient temples than love stories." Aunt Tempie winked at Florence. "I suppose I can spare a little time to tell you about our courtship. If you'd like."

"Oh, yes! Do, please." Florence tucked her hands in her lap and leaned forward eagerly. Jessica pulled the corners of her shawl together and twisted the ends.

"Very well. We met after my first Season in London. I was not a great success. Not like my dear friends." She smiled to herself, her eyes dimming with memory. "My family wasn't wealthy, and my dowry not particularly enticing. Which meant my mother despaired of ever finding me a match. But my father—oh, he was far more practical."

Aunt Tempie's tone changed, her words dry. "Father believed that anything might be accomplished if one had the right associates. So it was in the winter of 1773 that he invited a man to join us for Christmas. Mr. Thomas Bolingbrooke—a gentleman whose family grew wealthy building ships for the British armada." She chuckled. "I despised him the moment we met."

Jessica started, jerking her gaze from the fireplace to her look at Aunt Tempie. "You—you despised him?"

"But I thought you loved each other," Florence protested, her voice shocked and her eyes wide with betrayal. "Aunt Tempie, how horrible."

But their aunt continued to smile. "It was Christmas. Snow and ice mingled together, keeping everyone in the house for days. It gave Mr. Bolingbrooke more than enough time to size me up. Of course, I didn't know that at the time. I made a most favorable impression." She adjusted a pair of shears on the table. "But then I discovered what Thomas's purpose in my home meant. At nineteen, I detested war. I hated having my choices taken from me. And when my father presented me with a betrothed nearly a dozen years my senior, with thinning hair and not an inch taller than my own modest height, I thought my world had ended." She lowered her hands to her lap.

"That sounds...awful." Jessica couldn't think of another word for it. She rather wanted to offer her aunt a supportive embrace. But Aunt Tempie appeared perfectly at ease, which made Jessica uncertain. "Wasn't it awful?"

"At first. Because I made it so." The woman looked from one great-niece to the other. "I was determined to be miserable, and it took my poor Thomas some time to convince me otherwise. I am thankful that he did not give up on me. I was rather high-spirited as a girl. Much like you, Jessica."

"Me?" Jessica leaned back into the arm of the sofa. "I assure you, I am remarkably practical in nature."

"That is a lark," Florence said airily. "You are absolutely stubborn as a mule, Jessica. And then you become all gingery when you don't have your way."

The truth didn't smart. Much. Jessica aimed a crooked smile at her sister. "Very well. Maybe I am a little warm-blooded."

"As I said," Aunt Tempie continued with a lift to her eyebrows. "High-spirited." All three laughed before their great-aunt continued. "Thomas saw more than the cross, ungovernable girl I was. He came to me one day in the spring, after we had been married for months, mind you. He said he wished to travel, and as I possessed a will of iron, he thought he could bring me with him. I wasn't a delicate girl, but as fierce a woman as he had ever met."

She shook her head. "And then he took me to Switzerland. France. Prussia. Rome. Finally to Greece and Egypt."

"But when did you fall in love with him?" Florence asked, voice somewhat plaintive. "How long did it take?"

"The first time we embarked, I think." Aunt Tempie's eyes glowed with tears and memories. "We stood together at the side of the ship, bound for Calais. He covered my hand with his and he said, 'I cannot imagine undertaking this adventure without you, Temperance.' And I could feel the truth in his words. That he actually *wanted* me to be with him." Tears fell from her eyes, though a smile still graced her lips.

Jessica withdrew a handkerchief from her sleeve and pressed it into her great-aunt's hand.

"Thank you, dear." The elderly woman dabbed at her eyes. "That was when I had to examine myself. What had I done to deserve such a remark? Nothing, I assure you. But the man at my side had spent weeks and months showing me kindness in every possible way. He never rose to my sharp words, or my ill-conceived tricks. There were many of those, I assure you. I showed my displeasure in hundreds of tiny actions. Here I had thought to punish him when he only wanted to show me his love."

Jessica's chest tightened. She could see where her story and her aunt's might have similarities. Yet Ellis Webb wasn't a husband showing a wife that he cared for her. Ellis didn't do any more than tolerate Jessica's antics. He ignored her when he could. Yes, her aunt's story had ended with love, but Jessica didn't take it too much to heart.

"When it became clear we would never have children of our own," her aunt continued, her composure regained,

"I thought Thomas would put me aside. Leave me at home to my sorrow and empty nursery while he went on with his life. But he proved again how much he cared for me. Thomas never left me alone. We went everywhere together. We spoiled our nieces and nephews most terribly. Which is why your father is perfectly content to allow me to do the same for you two ladies."

Florence laughed, and Jessica allowed herself a smile.

"And now you see why romance and adventure are inseparable in my mind and heart." Aunt Temperance folded the handkerchief into a small square, placing it on the table before her. "They came into my life together and remained all the days that my Thomas stayed with me."

"You must miss him terribly," Florence said, rising from her chair and coming to sit on Aunt Tempie's other side. "I am so glad you came to be with us during Christmas. We would not have you be lonely, would we, Jessica?"

"Never," Jessica said with firmness. "Thank you for telling us about our great-uncle." Then she rose and drifted back to the window to look out at the world of white. If she imagined, only for a moment, standing at the rail of a ship with an ocean of possibility before her, she most certainly did *not* picture a man at her side. A man with dark eyes and a crooked smile. A man that looked disturbingly like Ellis Webb.

DEAR ESTHER

Brookfield House, Hatfield
December 23rd, 1815

My Dear Friend,

The longest nights of the year are upon us, and they have given me cause to feel maudlin. Yesterday, I recounted to my nieces how my dear Thomas and I met, married, and fell in love. You will remember how difficult those first months of marriage were for me—convinced as I was that I could never be happy with the man my father had chosen for me. How grateful I am now that Thomas was that man—and so patient with his impish young wife!

But I must not dwell so on things of the past. Not when there are delightful stirrings of romance in the present. Allow me to divert you with the happenings of this week. My eager niece, Florence, introduced me to her young man when he came to dinner earlier this week. He was all sweet hesitancy, and when he tried to speak to her, he could hardly say a word of sense. The gentleman is absolutely besotted, and he looks at her with such open admiration that I cannot see how their budding romance could fail.

My niece Jessica is another matter entirely. I watched her and the gentleman—Mr. Webb, he is called—covertly. They are like two thunderheads, destined to meet in a great clash of storms and lightning. They look at each other when the other isn't watching, eyes always searching for some sign they do not yet see. Then, when they speak, it is rather like watching two swordsmen prepare to duel. They sharpen their rapiers, size one another up, and take jabs at one another. I am most diverted while watching them dance about their feelings for one another—however complicated *those* must be. I find myself wondering what could have brought them to such a state.

Perhaps they will not be so easy to match as I thought. But I have great hopes for them. If they will ever uncross their swords long enough to see what is before them.

I have hopes that telling Jessica about my love with Thomas will stir her thoughts and her heart. Now, to work on the gentleman. I have secreted away a bit of mistletoe that Jessica prepared for the Christmas festivities. If I can place the berries and my great-niece in the same place at the same time, I may yet accomplish my matchmaking plan.

Have you heard word from Margarette? Since she began this scheme of matchmaking, I intend to tell her the whole of my experiences. You ought to write to Euota, if you have not. She has found herself a most delightful story of her own. I hope we may all meet again soon, so we might regale one another of how we spent this Christmas apart, yet as close in friendship as ever.

Yours,

Temperance

CHAPTER 7

Having three younger brothers, in addition to a younger sister, meant Jessica was forever being pulled along in one direction or another by enthusiastic younger siblings. Today, the snow had stopped. No sooner had she discovered that fact, standing at her bedroom window to take the temperature, then her youngest brother had pounded his fist upon her door.

Most unmannerly of him.

"Jess," Matthew called through the wood. "We are going to check the skating pond. Father said we could take the sleigh. Are you coming?"

Though Jessica counted herself a dignified woman on most occasions, the possibility of ice-skating transformed her with childlike delight. "Yes, of course!" She ran to the door and threw it open in time to see her brother dart away. "Don't you dare leave without me," she shouted at his retreating form. He waved a hand over his shoulder, then skidded to a stop in front of Florence's bedroom door to offer the same ill-mannered morning greeting.

Jessica shut her door and hurried to her closet. Though she had completed dressing for the day, she wasn't prepared to go out into the snow. This necessitated more layers made of wool, thick stockings, sturdy walking boots, and her skates, of course. The wooden flat with the metal blades fastened to the base waited for her at the bottom of her wardrobe.

When she came downstairs at last, with fur-lined mittens, cap, and muff, she met Florence and two of her three brothers. The front door burst open to reveal that Henry, all of sixteen years old, had already been outside. "I've fetched the sleigh. Everyone ready?"

From upstairs, their mother shouted down. "Absolutely no one may skate unless Florence says it is safe."

They all knew better than to groan, though Florence grinned broadly at them. "Yes, Mama." Though she was the second-eldest, she was also the safest of them all.

Not that the skating pond posed much of a threat. It was on the marquess's property, and he employed a local man to check the ice every year before allowing anyone upon it. If the man had approved the ice, he posted a blue flag beside a stone pit laden with dry wood. The skating pond was only three feet deep at its center. It froze quickly, and it froze hard.

The five Nettles climbed aboard the sleigh, with Robert taking up the horse's leads. The world around them, white and unspoilt, glittered in the weak morning sunlight.

Robert, Henry, and Matthew eagerly made plans for a race across the pond to warm themselves up for a game of hockey on the ice. Of all the games converted from land to pond in the winter, it was the boys' favorite. They had piled their curved sticks on the floor of the sleigh, and Matthew announced he had brought cork stoppers for the game.

"We need more people to play an interesting game," Henry reminded them. "Jess, will you play with us?"

"Certainly not." Jessica glared at her brother over her shoulder. She had placed herself on the front bench next to Robert. "The last time I tried to play with you lot, you kept purposefully hitting the bung beneath my skirts. That is hardly a dignified thing for young gentlemen to do."

Florence laughed. "You see why I gave up playing with them years ago."

"Quite right of you, too." Jess sniffed.

"Girls aren't any fun," Matthew muttered.

Jessica laughed along with Florence, who said cheerfully, "You will certainly change your opinion on that as you get older."

Matthew crossed his arms over his chest. "I doubt it."

They followed the slight indentations in the snow where the path through the woods lay, and soon enough found themselves at the edge of the pond. A blue flag had already been posted, and the boys sent up a cheer when Florence sat on a convenient tree stump to tie on her skates.

She was the most elegant on skates, a fact which Jessica well knew and admired. After Florence had the skates affixed to her boots, she went to the ice. In a moment, she was gliding, slowly and with care, around the edges of the pond. The boys held still, watching and waiting, their sticks in hand. Jessica sat on the stump and began work on her own skates.

Florence spiraled inward, a look of delight in her eyes when she arrived there. She looked up and waved at them. "No cracking or snapping ice here. I think we are safe to enjoy ourselves."

The boys cheered again, and a surprising, answering cheer came from the other side of the pond. Another sleigh emerged, this one driven by Franklin Thackery. His three half-brothers were with him in the sleigh, and Ellis Webb came through the trees behind them on a horse.

Jessica's spirits fell. She hadn't anticipated the Thackery family having the same idea as her brothers. But then, she supposed, most of the boys in the neighborhood would have already made plans to converge at the pond for their winter games.

Florence did not seem to mind. She had left the center of the pond to skate to the edge where the Thackery brothers worked to strap on their skates. She remained on the ice, apparently in conversation with them.

With a sigh, Jessica rose from her seat and stepped onto the ice. It took her a moment to accustom herself to the glide-step required to move across the frozen water. The ability came back to her, as it always did, by the time she reached the center of the pond. She hesitated. Did she join Florence at the edge, or pretend she did not care and enjoy her exercise?

Ellis had dismounted, and he approached the ice several feet away from where the Thackery brothers sat to strap on their skates, still leading his horse. Jessica made up her mind and skated toward him. When she was within speaking distance, she called to him, "Do you intend to skate, Mr. Webb?"

His expression remained solemn, his eyebrows raised.

"What could possibly induce me onto the ice, Miss Nettle? It is foolishness to spend one's time in the cold, on clumsy footwear, when one ought to be tucked up at home in a library. Before a roaring fire. With a book."

Jessica grinned at him and skated closer, her hands tucked in her muff. "I suppose if one isn't very good at skating, every alternative activity would be preferred."

"We both know that I am adequate at skating." He smirked, and the tilt to his lips brought out her scowl. He really ought not be allowed to look so charming *all* the time.

"Yes." She untucked one hand from her muff to gesture to the middle of the pond. "Adequate. Because I recall well a winter not too long ago when you landed so hard upon your tail-end that you broke through the layer of ice to the water beneath."

His laugh shocked her. An honest, deep laugh that rolled across the ice and brought the attention of the others upon them. When he paused for breath, his dark eyes alight with merriment, he sent a crooked smile toward her. "I cannot think of any lady ever mentioning my tail-end to me, Miss Nettle."

Her face warmed. In her excitement about skating, she had completely forgotten her decorum. And he had defended against her jest. Jessica wrinkled her nose at him, then turned and glided away. She was perfectly content to leave him on the shore.

Her brothers rushed by her on their skates, nearly upsetting her balance in their hurry. They clamored for the Thackerys and Ellis to join them in their game. The other boys had brought their sticks, and they hurried to divide into teams. But Franklin said he had rather not and joined Florence in skating around the edge of the pond instead. Florence brought him along with her to where Jessica made circles on the ice at the opposite end of the pond from Ellis.

Jessica watched them come with muted interest. If she wanted to pull them apart, she first had to make certain they did not belong together. Franklin skated alongside her sister quite well, and he did not touch her. He skated with both hands tucked behind his back and slowed to a stop when Florence did.

"This is my favorite winter exercise," Florence declared, her cheeks already a rosy shade. "There is no freedom like this, gliding across the ice."

Ellis still remained off the ice, but it appeared he was at least strapping on a pair of skates. She watched him a moment before realizing Franklin was in the midst of an extended attempt to agree with her sister.

"...absolutely liberating. One of my favorite things to do in winter. A game of hockey, or bowling on the ice never goes amiss either. But yes. Racing across the pond. It revives my spirits." He beamed at Florence, his eyes wide and eager, while she colored prettily.

This would never do.

Jessica skated in a wide arc around the couple. "I cannot recall seeing you at the pond at all last year." Then she stopped, barely between them. "In fact, I think your brothers and ours made a few disparaging remarks about your lack of enthusiasm for their usual games."

"Oh. Well. I—" Franklin tugged at the green woolen scarf around his throat. "Last winter, things were frightfully busy at home."

"Hm." She pushed forward on her feet again, glancing

at Florence over her shoulder to see her sister smiling sympathetically at Franklin.

Florence moved closer to him. "Duty can sometimes keep us from our own enjoyment."

Jessica narrowed her eyes at them both. He made excuses for an obvious exaggeration, and then she made excuses for him. But that wasn't love. How did she put them to the test?

"Yes. Exactly. Duty," Franklin said. "I am thankful that today, I have nowhere else to be but here." His enamored smile returned. "On the ice." The implication that he meant "with Florence" was obvious from the way he leaned toward her.

"A race," Jessica blurted. The besotted couple looked at her as one.

"What was that, Jessica?" Florence pulled her muff closer.

"I suggested we race. From one end of the pond to the other." She pointed to a large rock beside the pond near its end. "From here to the stone. The first one who passes the stone wins."

Ellis made his way across the ice toward them now, dodging their brothers as they slammed sticks into the ice in pursuit of the large cork they used in place of a ball. She grinned as she watched him trying to accustom himself to his skates for the first time in a year while in the middle of a pack of shouting boys. He nearly took a blow to his ankle but swerved in his path to avoid Peter's curved stick. The boys shouted as they fought for possession of the bung.

"I don't know that we need to race." Florence's protest, soft as it was, did not fool Jessica in the least.

Of their whole family, brothers included, Florence possessed the most talent on the ice. She skated like a dream when she tried for grace. She could cut letters into the ice so finely one might recognize her penmanship. And she had a knack for speed, too. On the ice, despite her skirts, she moved with purpose and rhythm that propelled her ahead of anyone who dared challenge her.

"You are too modest, Florence." Jessica turned pointedly to Franklin, who appeared puzzled by this proposal. "You will race, will you not, Mr. Thackery? Since you are so fond of ice skating, I know you cannot resist an opportunity to rush full speed across the pond."

Ellis slowed to a stop beside them. "What's this about a race?" He rubbed his gloved hands together, wincing as he did. "Monstrously cold out here, isn't it?"

Since he had promised to help her, Jessica couldn't allow her irritation with Ellis to show. Instead, she gave him a friendly smile. A coaxing one, she hoped. "I am trying to convince your cousin and my sister to take part in a friendly race. From here to where that rock marks the opposite end of the pond." She pointed, and Ellis blew on his hands as he followed the gesture.

"You want the four of us to race? Men and women together?" He tossed the long end of his gray scarf over his shoulder. "That doesn't seem fair."

"Why?" she challenged. "Do you think the men will out-distance us?"

"Naturally." Ellis grinned at her. "But I've no objection to proving my theory." He tugged his hat down tighter upon his head. "Do you, Frank?"

Franklin hedged. "It does not seem polite."

"And what if we win?" Jessica challenged before

Florence could offer any agreement with Frank. "In the unlikely event that either Florence or I outpace you gentlemen?"

Ellis's smile turned devious. He could not know that Florence would win. Yet he had sensed Jessica had a plan. "I should think we pay a forfeit."

"Too right." Jessica looked at her sister and raised her eyebrows. "What should we play for, dear? Knowing, of course, that you cannot possibly win against these gentlemen, what prize would you claim if you could?"

"Go on, Miss Florence. What might you wager? The first dance at the marquess's ball?" Franklin laughed, adopting a teasing tone, his words the words of a man who had already calculated his own winnings. "Perhaps the loser must wear a sign of their humiliation to the Christmas party."

And for the first time in ages, Florence frowned. Deeply. "You are quite confident in your skills, sir. Or do you merely doubt mine?"

Franklin sobered, eyes going wide with fear. "No. Not at all. That is, I am certain you are quite an accomplished —er—that is, you likely possess talent when it comes to skating."

"Indeed." Florence put her nose in the air. "If a lady wins the race, the gentlemen must wear sprigs of holly in their hats to services on Sunday. If a gentleman wins, the ladies will wear unadorned bonnets. I think that is suitable enough."

Jessica grinned with delight. Florence had spent a great deal of time decorating her bonnet for the Christmas Eve service. It was a beautiful work of art. One she wouldn't risk unless she intended to win. That meant her sister would not throw the race in order to preserve Franklin's pride.

Robert broke from his game long enough to start them. Other women might demure from racing gentlemen—it could hardly be considered a lady-like thing to challenge potential suitors to race across a pond —but not Florence. And certainly not Jessica. Besides, they had known both gentlemen far too long to be missish about a friendly exercise.

When Robert gave the shout to go, all four young adults took off. Jessica's eyes were on her sister as Florence pulled away, arms moving in concert with her legs to keep her balanced. Ellis and Franklin gasped and gave forth greater effort, but far too late. Florence reached the finish, then Ellis, then Franklin, and Jessica happily brought up the rear. It took reminding herself of maidenly modesty to not crow over her sister's victory the way one of their brothers would.

Heart still pounding from the exertion, Jessica had to grin at the look on Franklin's face as Florence twirled in a triumphant circle. She had won. Bested both gentlemen. It might not test their love, but it would certainly test Franklin's pride. A woman could beat few men—at anything—and have a gentleman still wish to pay court to her. The next moment would reveal something of the man's character, and Franklin's hat on Sunday would garner attention and comment enough that the days after would be equally revealing. Could he harbor affection for a woman who bested him in a race?

Franklin bent, hands on his thighs, as he took in great gulps of air. Then he lifted his head and stared at Florence, incredulously. She stopped her twirling and looked at him, the smile on her face fading swiftly under his study. Her hands fell demurely to her sides.

"That," Franklin said, voice deepening, "was an incredible display. How did you move with such speed?" He stood to his full height and held his gloved hand out to her. "That was marvelous, Miss Florence. You must teach me that skill. Or will you tell me it all comes down to practice?"

A glow appeared in Florence's eyes, her whole face illuminated with her smile.

Jessica did not get to see more, however. A hand on her wrist, and a quick tug, had her whirled around on the ice and in Ellis's control. He tucked her arm through his, pulled her tightly against his side, and propelled them both away from the scene playing out between the couple.

"Mr. Webb," she protested, trying to look over her shoulder.

Ellis switched direction, thwarting her. She grumbled but faced forward again. They were going back to where they had started the race. Good. She could collect her muff.

"That did not go as you expected, did it?"

She looked up at him, getting an excellent view of his profile. Sharp nose. Strong chin. Long, thick lashes framing his dark eyes. And a superior smirk upon his lips. Horrid man.

"Not at all," she said. "Either Mr. Thackery is an exceptional actor, or he truly does not mind that my sister trounced him in a race."

"I have known my cousin all his life." Ellis looked down at her, their gazes colliding with the usual electric jolt she expected when they were at odds. Except. They were not at odds. And the jolt made her fingers and toes tingle with pleasure rather than irritation. "Frank has no talent for acting. I am certain he did not mind your sister besting him at all."

Jessica had to look away from him. She most certainly would not tolerate another moment of his smirk. "Then he is singular among men."

Ellis chuckled, and he curved their path away from her muff. She watched as they sailed past her warm accessory. Was he testing her? Did he think she would break away and go fetch her possession? She tucked herself more securely to his side instead.

"Frank is a good chap, I'll grant you. But I do not think his sort is so rare as you seem to believe."

Jessica clicked her tongue against the roof of her mouth. "Well. Would *you* mind a lady proving superior to you in a physical challenge?" He did not answer right away, and for some reason, this made her heart fall. She looked up at him, ready to claim victory in her supposition. He wasn't looking at her. He stared straight ahead, but the tension in his brow and jaw told her he was deep in thought.

"Ellis?"

He shrugged, and she felt the movement through her shoulder and arm pressed to his. "It would depend on the lady, I think." He looked down at her, and she avoided his gaze, uncertain of what she might see in his eyes.

They skated in silence until they came back around the pond again to where her muff remained on the edge of the ice. Franklin and Florence were there, Florence collecting her things, too. After Jessica tucked her hands securely in her muff, she left all three of them behind, talking of the men's forfeit and where they might find holly for their hatbands.

An unfortunate effect of her agreement with Ellis meant two things. She and he had a secret. And secrets shared meant they had a new level of understanding between them. One thing Jessica absolutely could not do was mistake that understanding for something more. She had already made that error once, and it had caused her humiliation and heartbreak. She wasn't about to let Ellis Webb hurt her a second time.

CHAPTER 8

ELLIS AND FRANKLIN JOINED THE YOUNGER BOYS FOR A round of their hockey game. The lads had already exhausted themselves, which gave the men a questionable advantage. After nearly two hours on the ice, Florence and Jessica declared it time to return home. They had watched the game, calling out encouragement to their brothers and Franklin's half-brothers alike.

Everyone sat on stumps, logs, and the ice itself to unbuckle the straps from their boots and remove the blades. The ladies helped one another with the somewhat awkward task.

It took effort for Ellis to keep his eyes off of Jessica throughout. Though he had wished in years past that she did not regard him with such disdain, the desire had increased with each moment in her presence. As did the temptation to ask her outright why their easy friendship had ended. Had it only been a matter of age? When he left for university, did that require an uncomfortable barrier to grow between them?

After Ellis untethered his horse from the branch where he'd secured it, he wandered to the Nettle sleigh. Franklin stood beside it, looking down into Miss Florence's eyes. Jessica was on the other side, instructing her brothers to move their sticks out of the way of her seat.

Ellis came alongside her. "Miss Nettle." She turned around, and he noted several dark curls had fallen from her fur-lined bonnet and draped down across her scarf. His fingers twitched as he tried to ignore the desire to tuck those curls back into place. "I regret that our enjoyable morning must come to an end."

Her eyebrows raised, and she looked over her shoulder to Franklin and her sister. "You did not hear? My sister has invited all the Thackerys back to our home for warm cider. Doubtless our brothers will keep Mr. Thackery's brothers as prisoners for as long as possible." She faced Ellis again and tipped her head. "One would assume the invitation included you, Mr. Webb, given that you are a member of their party."

"Indeed." He lowered his voice and bent to speak more directly in her ear. "You do not seem pleased by this development, Miss Nettle. Why not look at it as an opportunity to extend your testing of our happy couple?"

Jessica glowered at him and opened her mouth to respond when her youngest brother, Matthew, said, "Are you coming in our sleigh or not, Jess? Florence already joined the Thackerys."

"She did what?" Jessica spun around, and Ellis looked over her head to the other sleigh. At that exact moment, Franklin assisted Jessica into the front seat of the sleigh. Jessica made a sound of distress even as Ellis chuckled.

She turned around and swatted his shoulder with a mittened hand. "It isn't the least bit amusing, Ellis Webb."

He caught her hand before she could tuck it again in her muff. "I beg to differ, Jessica Nettle. Come now. In the sleigh you go, or they will be off without us."

Her expression changed to one of suspicion, but she did not yank her hand away from his as he expected. Instead, she allowed him to hold it until she had stepped into her family's sleigh. She settled on the bench seat, then gave him one last superior look. "Are you coming to our home, Mr. Webb?"

Her tone did nothing to dissuade him. "I could never turn down such a heartfelt invitation." He dared wink at her, and she rewarded his audacity with an exasperated sigh. But he caught the slightest lift to her lips, the barest twinkle in her eye. Then Robert Nettle shouted to the horses, and the sleigh pulled away for the path through the trees that would deliver the Nettles home.

Ellis mounted and followed, catching up to them with ease. A groom waited at the front of the house for their return, and soon all the animals were taken in hand for a trip to the warm barn. One at a time, the men and boys scraped their boots before entering the foyer of Brookfield House. Mrs. Nettle and the great-aunt, Mrs. Bolingbrooke, came into the hall to see what all the noise was about.

"It was a dandy of a time, Mother," Matthew exclaimed, his youthful voice carrying over everyone else's. Florence had moved to her great aunt, likely explaining the invitation. The Thackery and Nettle boys were clamoring for biscuits and cider. Franklin stood near Florence, gazing at her with his usual admiration.

Standing nearest the door, Ellis skirted his way around

the boisterous young men until he stood behind Jessica. She had removed her bonnet and mittens but struggled with the buttons of her coat. When they came free at last, she started to shrug it off.

With both hands at her shoulders, Ellis caught her coat and helped slide it from her arms. Jessica stood still as a statue as he handed the article of clothing the harried-looking butler. Then she peered over her shoulder at him. "Thank you."

"Not at all." He took his coat off, then started unwinding the scarf around his neck. Every time he touched her, even for so simple a thing as to hand her into the sleigh, Ellis's thoughts and feelings shifted. He did not want her grudging truce. Not anymore. Instead, he wanted her friendship, returned to him as fully as it had been before he'd grown up and it had disappeared.

"You put yourself in danger, sir." Jessica spoke with lowered voice and tilted head. "Do you remember what happened the last time you left your coat in our home unattended?"

He froze mid-motion, his scarf dangling from his hand. "That was you?" The year before, he had visited the Nettle family with his uncle, Mr. Thackery. He had worn his coat home without putting his hands in any of the pockets. Days later, his valet had informed him household vermin had attacked his favorite coat. Mice had eaten their way through his pockets, leaving his coat quite destroyed.

They had never determined why such a thing would happen. His valet had theorized that Ellis had left biscuit crumbs in his pockets, a sin that Ellis still vehemently denied.

"I ought to have known. However did you manage it?"

She batted her eyes at him, and rather than say anything cross, Ellis barked a laugh. Jessica smirked and walked away, following the others into a downstairs sitting room. Ellis brought up the rear of the party.

The large, welcoming room had all its curtains open to allow the winter sunlight inside. A large fire burned in the hearth, and the boys immediately jostled for the best position to stand in front of the flames. They were already recounting their prowess in the games of the morning.

Jessica and her sister sat on a long couch, and Franklin joined them there. That left Ellis to find a chair near his cousin to wait for the refreshments. He settled in nicely and put his feet up on a footstool. The moment he did, a small dog crawled from beneath the furniture. It yipped at him, then jumped into Ellis's lap before he was fully aware what it intended.

"Mutton, no." Jessica jumped up and came to snatch the dog from him, putting it on the floor gently. "We do not jump on our guests."

He chuckled and held his hand out to the little dog. "I don't mind in the slightest, Miss Nettle."

"Then your manners are no better than his," she said, pointing at the terrier. "Mutton belongs to my Aunt Temperance. He is an incorrigible beastie."

"Perhaps so, but then, so am I." He gave his knee a pat, and the dog leapt up into his lap again before turning around to grin at Jessica. "You see? We are perfect company for each other." He scratched the animal behind his ears, and the dog tilted his head into Ellis's hand.

"Next you will be feeding him biscuits." Jessica went back to her seat on the couch. The next half hour passed with conversation and refreshment. Warm cider, biscuits, and sandwiches came out from the kitchens. Mrs. Nettle tutted all over them and insisted her sons tell her all about their morning. Then Mr. Nettle appeared, settling in a seat near the fire. He peppered Franklin with questions about their father, tenants, and any other news the Thackery family might have.

Ellis sat in near silence, scratching the little dog in his lap. At some point, Mutton jumped down and left him. It seemed the animal had decided to explore the ground in search of any biscuit crumbs or sandwich leavings. The room grew quiet as the boys filed out in search of some other fun. Ellis leaned his head back in the chair and stared into the fire, entering a comfortable doze.

Until someone put a hand on Ellis's shoulder. He startled awake and looked up into the green-ringed eyes of Jessica Nettle. They reflected blue firelight down at him, and Ellis had to swallow back the urge to tell her how much he admired her eyes.

"Have you seen Mutton?" she asked, and his befuddled mind took several moments to understand the question.

"The little dog? No. Not since he left me to scavenge the carpets." He lowered his feet from the footstool, then looked up at the mantel clock. An hour had passed since their arrival. Which meant he had been sleeping for at least half that time.

Jessica bit her lip and looked away from him, and Ellis realized they were in the room alone.

"Where did everyone go?" he asked somewhat blearily. He put both hands on the arms of the chair to push himself to his feet. Standing, he was suddenly much nearer Jessica. Less than an arm's length of air separated them.

"The boys are in the billiard room. My mother, aunt, and sister are showing Mr. Thackery the decorations in the gallery." She put her chin out, her gaze sharpening. "You are supposed to help me to dissuade Florence and Franklin from forming an attachment, yet here you are. Sleeping."

Ellis had to cover a yawn, which made Jessica's glare turn icy. He decided to glower right back at her. "I cannot help that the morning wore on me."

"Are you a man of five-and-sixty or six-and-twenty?" she demanded, folding her arms. "Honestly, Mr. Webb. If you are going to laze about, what use are you?"

He opened his mouth to counter her argument, when a more delightful thought took hold. He pressed his lips together and mirrored her stance, crossing his arms, but cocked his head to one side to study her. "I find it interesting that my short nap has caused you such distress. You cannot mean to imply, Miss Nettle, that you actually *need* my help?"

Her nose wrinkled. "Need?" She scoffed. "I need your help as much as I need a toothache, sir."

"Really?" He leaned toward her, lowering his voice. "Then why did you wake me, if you do not need me?"

Her eyes narrowed, and she shifted closer, apparently not at all cowed by his proximity. "You overestimate your importance on all accounts, sir."

"Do I?" He studied the green and blue of her eyes, noting their brightness with admiration. Then his gaze dipped lower, where her lips pressed together until they pushed slightly outward. Pursed. Disapproving. Entirely kissable.

She swallowed, and Ellis caught his breath.

"Mutton!"

Ellis and Jessica both stepped back, and he jerked his gaze to the open door. The shout had come from the corridor.

"Mutton?" It was Florence. She appeared a moment later, her hands on either side of the doorway. She leaned into the room, her eyes wide and worried. "Jessica, have you seen Mutton? We cannot find him anywhere. Aunt Tempie is quite worried."

Jessica shook her head. "I came here to look for him myself, but he's not here."

Franklin appeared behind Miss Florence, peering over the young lady's shoulder. When he saw Jessica and Ellis together, his eyebrows contracted sharply. Ellis hurried forward, babbling, not wanting to give Franklin the ability to say a word on the awkward scene.

"No, I have not seen him in this room since we had refreshments. When did she last have him?"

Miss Florence pursed her lips. "When we were all in this room together. Aunt Tempie thought he followed her out when we went to look at the greenery, but I do not recall having him with us at all."

"Nor do I," Franklin said, a suspicious gleam yet in his eye. "I hoped we'd find the little fellow in here, napping with you. Or following Miss Nettle about."

Jessica shook her head. "As I said, I have not seen him."

A scuffle in the hall announced the arrival of Mrs.

Bolingbrooke to the scene. The elderly woman's bright eyes were wide with alarm. "Any luck, Florence?"

"No, Aunt. They haven't seen him."

Mrs. Bolingbrooke came fully into the room, her eyes darting about as though she might find the dog where the others had not. "My poor Mutton." She placed a hand over her heart and sat in a chair. "Wherever could he be? Sometimes he runs off at home. He is always in one scrape or another, much like a small child, but he always comes when I call."

Jessica stood beside her aunt's chair, laying a hand upon her shoulder. "He is a tiny dog in a new place. I doubt he went far, even if he is exploring." Then Jessica looked up, imploringly. At Ellis.

He did not even stop to consider why she thought he would know what to say and do. Instead, he turned around to address Franklin and Miss Florence. "We need to check all the rooms. Perhaps he ventured somewhere and trapped himself in a cupboard or closet."

Florence gasped and looked at her sister. "Jessica, the conservatory doors have been open all afternoon with the servants bringing in the evergreen boughs. What if the dog ran outside?"

Their great-aunt came to her feet. "If he wanders far, he won't know his way back. The grounds are still unfamiliar to him."

Jessica took her aunt's hand, speaking earnestly to her. "Please, Aunt Tempie. Sit down. You should stay right here in case he comes looking for you."

"Franklin and I will search the gardens," Ellis said. "Miss Nettle and Miss Florence can continue the search indoors." Ellis managed to take two steps toward the door before Mrs. Bolingbrooke spoke.

"No, that will never do." She removed a handkerchief from her long sleeve and dabbed at her eyes. Eyes he had thought were dry a moment ago. "Mutton isn't overly fond of strangers. He will not come if an unknown gentleman calls him."

"But he likes Florence and me." Jessica helped her aunt sink back into her chair. "We will divide into search parties." Jessica turned to her sister. "You keep looking in the house. I will check the gardens at once." She brushed by Ellis on the way out the door.

Mrs. Bolingbrooke dipped her head, the bit of lace still before her eyes. "She will need help." Then she looked up at Ellis, eyes glimmering but quite clear. "Florence and Mr. Thackery can continue the search in the house and enlist the boys' help. Will you go with my great-niece outside, Mr. Webb?"

"Of course, Mrs. Bolingbrooke."

He should have sent Franklin out of doors. But given the way Franklin stared at him, with an almost gleeful smile upon his face, his friend had an entirely ridiculous thought in his head. A thought about Ellis and Jessica, unless Ellis missed his guess.

It would be far safer for him to trail after Jessica than stay anywhere near Franklin.

"Dashed inquisitive dog," he muttered, rubbing at the back of his neck as he stormed down the hallway, boots stomping on the tile.

He met Jessica near the door, where she looked at him with some surprise. He didn't let her ask. "I am coming outside with you."

Though he expected her to protest, Jessica's shoulders relaxed immediately, though she directed a strained smile toward him. "Thank you. My aunt adores that little dog. He was a gift from her late husband."

That put a finer point on the sudden furor of looking for the little beast. No stranger to the importance of animal companions, Ellis did not delay in leaving the room to find his coat. A footman helped him into it, then handed Ellis his hat and gloves before performing the same service for Jessica. The two of them went out the door and around the walkway to the side of the house where the conservatory met the gardens.

"The servants will have churned the snow up with all their comings and goings, but keep a lookout for any small prints that might belong to the dog." Ellis swept the gardens with a glance. Though no hedges grew above his waist, a little white dog might easily go unseen in a world covered with snow. Why did the dog have to be white?

They set about calling for the animal, and Ellis whistled several times. They walked along the side of the house where the doors to the conservatory had been open. Then they walked farther out, between hedges and through the cold garden.

Until they heard a bark in the distance.

"That must be him!" Jessica wound her way along the garden paths, making her way toward the stables. "Did you hear? It sounded like a little dog barking, did it not?" She did not take the time to look over her shoulder to check that Ellis followed. Instead, Jessica burst from the garden path the moment she was free of the shrubbery. She started off across the meadow, her boots sinking into the snow as she went.

The clump of heavier footfall behind announced Ellis before he said, "Slow down, Jessica. You might fall into a drift."

True, the meadow was not perfectly flat. There were quite a few dips in the land. But then— "Did you call me by my Christian name, sir?" She stopped her awkward walk and turned around, not bothering to hide her surprise. "You have not done that since I was a child."

He stumbled to a stop, his breath misting before him in the cold. "Forgive me, Miss Nettle. A mere slip of the tongue. Old habits, and all that." He arched his eyebrows at her, then kept walking as though he would move past her. Jessica started walking again when he drew even with her, and immediately envied the sturdiness of his boots and the length of his legs. He made passing through the snow appear much easier than she did.

"You ought not let such a slip happen again," she murmured, her voice pitched low so it would not carry far through the cold. "It would give people the wrong idea."

Ellis said nothing. The crunch of snow beneath their feet was the only sound. Snowfall began, the white dusting coming from the gray above further muting the world. Jessica nearly sighed with relief when her feet hit the gravel scattered around the stable. She called for Mutton again. Ellis whistled.

The top half of the stable door opened, and a groom peered out at them. "Something wrong, Miss Nettle?" the lad called.

"My aunt lost her dog," Jessica answered, voice raised to carry. "Has a little white terrier come out here?"

The lad shook his head and opened the bottom door to the stable, too. He came out, and a carriage dog followed with two small puppies beside her. One yipped. Had that been the bark she'd heard before? Jessica turned to Ellis, not for the first time, hoping for his help. Though why it felt so natural to look to him, she had no wish to examine.

"Would you and some of your fellows look about for him?" Ellis asked the groom. Then he looked down at Jessica, a sympathetic light in his eyes. "I doubt he went farther than the stable yard."

"Yes, sir. We'll search him out."

Ellis's expression returned to its usual seriousness. Furrowed brow. Darkened eyes. A tense set to his chin. "Good fellow. If any of the lads find him, I will pay out a reward."

The groom bowed and disappeared back into the stable, likely to don a coat and rouse anyone else in the building to search for the wayward animal. Ellis turned around, his eyes sweeping across the direction they had come from. "We should go back and look around the house again, away from the gardens."

Though her gown's hem had grown heavy with snow, Jessica nodded once with determination before stepping toward the meadow. Ellis's hand stayed her when he touched her arm.

"We can take the path up to the house, Miss Nettle." He looked down at her dress, likely noting the darkened, wet fabric. "It will be easier on both of us."

She joined him, and they resumed calling for the lost

dog. Jessica could only imagine her aunt's distress if the poor creature did not turn up soon. As one of the last gifts from Aunt Tempie's late husband, Mutton held more significance for the woman than most pets would. Losing the dog so soon after Mr. Bolingbrooke's death would hurt her aunt deeply.

Gravel crunched beneath their boots. Going uphill wasn't nearly so easy as down. The falling snow floated down leisurely, the clouds in no great hurry to release their burden.

Ellis slipped on an icy rock, and his hands flailed. Jessica grabbed hold of his arm, helping him catch his balance. To his credit, he dipped his head in thanks as she removed her hands. "Dangerous work, that. I might've taken you down with me."

She caught herself smiling, a teasing word on the tip of her tongue. She swallowed it back. Frowned. "Be careful." Then she kept trudging up the gentle incline to the house. They were nearly there.

"Miss Nettle?" Ellis easily regained his place at her side, his longer legs eating up the ground far faster than her skirted steps.

"Yes, Mr. Webb?" She did not hide her impatience with him. Them. The whole situation of a missing dog that had forced them outside, together.

"When did our friendship end?"

Jessica stumbled, and this time, his hands caught her. His left hand at her lower back, his right going around her arm. Steadying her. Standing so near, her shoulder brushed his chest. She pulled in a quick breath, catching the scent of the bergamot and cedarwood of Ellis's cologne. She knew the scent quite well from a trick she had played on him—when she had replaced the liquid of his elegant bottle from Truefitt and Hill with vinegar.

She did not look up at him. She had no desire to see the expression he wore. She pulled her arm carefully away and continued up the hill. "I do not know what you mean."

"I think you do." He stayed walking beside her, but she tilted her head just enough so her bonnet shielded her face from his view. "There was a time when we laughed together, and we spent time in one another's company pleasantly. We went from that companionable existence to one in which I had to look over my shoulder whenever you were near, lest you drop a tin of spiders beneath my collar."

There had only been *two* spider incidents. The stringed creature and then she had drawn a spider, in ink, upon his pillow when he stayed at his cousin's home. A tiny thing. But if one did not look carefully, it could easily be mistaken as an actual creature.

"A man with the surname of Webb should not be so averse to spiders," she muttered, still walking. Still avoiding looking at him.

"And a woman with the surname of Nettle should avoid acting prickly as a hedgehog."

She stopped walking and turned to face him, but the sharp retort she meant to give never passed her lips. Because Ellis did not appear cross. Instead, sorrow pulled at the corners of his mouth, and his brow wrinkled with concern.

"I have never had an enemy before you, who I counted as a friend."

Her breath stuttered in her chest, and for the first time

in years, guilt squeezed her heart. He had always born her teasing and her tricks with an amiable smile or a laugh. Sometimes he ignored her entirely. Others, he mocked her antics.

But she staved off the guilt with one cold, awful thought. The moment that had held so much significance for her that it had changed forever how she acted toward him—he did not even remember it. She had planned the moment she revealed her affection for him with such precision and girlhood hope. And he had laughed and left her alone beneath the mistletoe.

She had stood still too long. Stared into his eyes too intently. His eyebrows pulled together tightly. His study of her increased as his gaze grew more penetrating.

Enemy, he had called her. The word stung.

"I really do not think this is the time or place for such a discussion." She tore her gaze from his. "We must find Mutton." And she marched away, clutching at her skirts with her mittened hands to hide how they trembled.

This time, Ellis did not continue at her side. He stayed several paces behind. When they at last arrived at the house, a window above them opened. Florence leaned out of it.

"There you are, Jessica." Florence's cheeks were a warm shade of rose, and her eyes danced merrily. "We found Mutton. He was asleep on the windowsill in Aunt Temperance's room, with the curtains drawn. No one could see him, and he did not hear our aunt's calls." She beamed as though she had just announced that Father Christmas himself had come to visit. "Mr. Webb, hurry inside. You two must be frozen." Then she swung the window closed.

Jessica shook her head and went to the door, ignoring the man behind her. She did not return to the sitting room for refreshment. Instead, the moment she was free of coat and bonnet, she went straight to her room without taking leave of anyone. Though she did turn at the top of the stairs to look back at Ellis. He stood at the foot of the stairs, staring up at her, looking completely perplexed.

When she obtained the privacy of her room, the thought finally dawned upon Jessica that Mutton never gone missing at all. He had certainly followed their aunt out of the sitting room and up to her bedroom. Which meant Aunt Temperance had to have known she left him there, the door closed, before she asked for the others to begin their search.

With a groan, Jessica fell backward onto her bed. "What a horrible sneak you are, Aunt Tempie. Sending off Franklin and Florence like that, and keeping Ellis and me out of your way by sending us outside." Still, she had to smile after a moment more of consideration. She had to admire Aunt Tempie's excessive cleverness. Even if it meant she needed to work twice as hard to undo her aunt's work.

She spent her afternoon considering all the ways in which she might yet prove to Florence that Franklin Thackery was not the husband for her, but her plans were interrupted time and time again by the memories of Ellis in the sitting room when he had leaned toward her as they stood alone. As she had always imagined he would lean in for the mistletoe kiss that never occurred.

CHAPTER 9

"I think you like her."

Ellis looked up from the book in his hands. Christmas Eve had arrived, and Sunday morning services with it. As usual, Ellis was the first of the men prepared for the day. However, that preparation did not extend to his cousin bursting into the room announcing Ellis *liked* someone. "You will have to be more specific, Frank." Ellis turned a page in his book and ignored his cousin.

Even though he knew precisely who Franklin meant.

"Bah." Franklin moved to the fire, holding his bare hands out to it. "I cannot abide the cold. Or this drafty house."

"For a three-hundred-year-old stone building, it isn't as drafty as one might think." Ellis smirked into his book. "And think of the history surrounding you."

"History?" Franklin snorted. "I would rather focus on the present and your avoidance of the topic at hand. You *like* Miss Jessica Nettle."

"I suppose so." Ellis kept his response languid, uninterested. "As much as I like anyone who shoves icicles into my coat, eggs in my boots, garden snakes in my bureau, and hides all my left shoes in the attic."

"Childish antics, to be sure, but—"

"Childish?" Ellis snapped his book closed, some of his ire with Jessica coming out in his voice. "Less than a year has passed since the last time she attempted to assassinate me."

"Pepper in your tea is not the same thing as poison."

"How helpful of you to point that out." Ellis dropped the book on the table beside his chair. "She was not always such an imp."

"I know." Franklin turned his back to the fire and folded his arms, pinning Ellis in place with his stare. "I was there, Cousin. She followed the two of us from one thing to the next, never caring if she tore the hem of her gown or lost a slipper in our adventures. And then we grew up."

Ellis steepled his fingers together before him and tilted his head to the side. "Is that when she grew to hate me?" he asked, tone thoughtful. "It was after I traveled Europe, was it not?"

Franklin shrugged. "I never bothered to pinpoint the moment she stopped looking at you with adoration and tried to scare you out of your wits. But I always found her attempts amusing." Then his grin widened. "Admit it. You usually did, too."

"Usually." Ellis didn't bother hiding his smirk.

"You do like her. Admit it."

"I would like her much better if she stopped treating me like an unwanted guest."

"You and she appeared to be getting along at the

pond yesterday morning." Franklin grinned in triumph. "And Miss Nettle did not unsettle you even once. She seemed perfectly amiable. And I saw you smiling. Several times."

With an impatient snort, Ellis pushed himself out of the chair. "Smile? Me? And ruin a perfectly good glower?" He walked over to a mirror on the wall and pretended to adjust his cravat. "Never."

The door burst open, this time admitting twelve-year-old James into the room. "Here you two are. Father says it is time to leave. The sleighs are outside."

"Ah, attending Sunday service in a sleigh. On Christmas Eve, no less." Franklin clapped Ellis on the back as he passed by on his way out the door. "We are in for a wonderful day."

Ellis shook his head, then took one last look at himself in the mirror. He pushed a stray lock of hair away from his forehead and met his own stare. Then he swallowed. Because Franklin had seen through him far too easily. Ellis liked Jessica. More than liked, which was dangerous. He admired her. He found her pretty and intelligent. Their truce allowed him nearer to her than he'd been in years. And what he observed of her made unfamiliar feelings stir within *him*.

He struggled with those feelings all the way to the little church where the neighborhood assembled for morning prayer and holy communion. A choir would sing carols and psalms. For an hour or more, Ellis could sit in peace and think on the importance of the coming day. Christmas. A time when all made merry, celebrating life and light. Remembering together the events that had taken place in Bethlehem long ago, when a child was born, and grew to proclaim peace on earth and goodwill toward man.

When they arrived at the church where Ellis had visited many times with his uncle and cousin, they slid into the family pew. And while the young men jostled for seats, Ellis waited calmly to enter the row himself. Up until the moment he realized the three younger Thackery men left him with one place to sit—directly behind the woman he desperately wanted to put from his mind.

The Nettle family sat in the pew in front of the Thackerys, as they always had. And the lovely white bonnet Jessica wore had ribbons trailing down her back. Her slender neck arched as she reached for a prayer book. A honey-blonde curl brushed her shoulder.

With Jessica sitting in front of him, his hopes for a peaceful hour spent in contemplation of scripture and ancient traditions vanished altogether. Because he knew, with no doubt, that he would spend the whole of his time pondering Jessica Nettle's disdain and trying to determine how to make things right between them once more. Not because he nursed any kind of hidden affection for her, of course. Franklin could crow about such a thing until he turned blue, but Ellis would never admit to anything as unfortunate as harboring feelings for a woman who clearly disliked him.

First, he needed to determine exactly why he fell out of favor with her. Stretching back through his memories, he could not recall the moment things had changed. Likely because her harmless jests from childhood had slowly become more...prickly.

When she was fourteen, and he eighteen, she had delighted in following him about in the summer. He was always with Franklin, and the two of them thought nothing of having a girl show them both what amounted to hero worship. She had delighted them with her quick wit, and she had proven herself amusing rather than annoying.

Once, he had teased her about the flowers in her bonnet. The next time he put on his hat, flowers appeared around its brim, held in place with a bright yellow ribbon. A harmless, fanciful thing. More than a year later, he had put on a hat to find Miss Nettle had lined the insides edge with blue ink. It had left an interesting circle on his skin and hair that took him days to wash away properly.

But between the summers of his eighteenth and twentieth year, a shift had occurred. What had caused it?

During one congregational hymn, he dared to lean forward to speak to her. The voices raised in song covered his words well. "You look lovely today, Miss Nettle."

Her shoulders tightened. She lifted her hymnal higher. Then she turned her head just enough for him to see her profile beneath the brim of her bonnet. Suspicion tightened her lips and arched her brow. She gave the slightest nod before she turned fully forward again.

Did that nod mark a point in his favor? Perhaps. And perhaps he could do more.

When the last hymn drifted away, and they said the final amens, Jessica slipped from the pew without saying a word to Ellis. He had startled her with his strangely timed compliment. What could he mean by speaking to her thus, and in public? Her looks had nothing to do with their truce.

Somehow, her declaration that she would ceasefire in order to ally with him temporarily had been interpreted as an invitation to act *friendly* toward her. A most dangerous thing. Especially given how much she disliked the idea of being Ellis's friend. The man was perpetually grumpy, and far too prone to brood. What sane woman would want to converse with him? Even if he was well traveled, well read, and...well...handsome.

Not that she thought about his looks often. No. She kept her thoughts upon his character. Which she hadn't examined closely in some time, come to think on it.

Before making her way out of the church and into the cold outside, Jessica stopped to speak to Mrs. Goodwin. The elderly woman perked up when Jessica sat next to her to exchange a few words about the sermon. "And will you be going to your son's home for Christmas dinner?" she asked, knowing that was the highlight of the widow's year.

"Oh, of course. He fetches me this afternoon. The dear boy. He has seven children, you know, and I think he means to tell me that his wife is due to have another."

"How marvelous for you, Mrs. Goodwin. I do hope you spoil them with sweets and stories, as you always did me." Jessica had held the esteemed lady, wife of their former apothecary, in high regard since childhood. She still kept a small shop, selling wares primarily of interest to women. Her home was small and comfortable. The one she had shared with her husband all their married life. Perhaps someday, she would agree to live with her son and his large brood.

"They are my greatest joy. But, my dear Miss Nettle, when will we hear an announcement about you?"

Jessica laughed, though the subject of her unmarried state had begun to sting in recent months. "Not yet, Mrs. Goodwin. I promise, if I ever find a man as wonderful as your Mr. Goodwin, I will snatch him up at once."

"Good girl." She patted Jessica on the hand. "Now, off with you. It is Christmas Eve, and I am certain there are many waiting to give you their best wishes."

Squeezing the older woman's hands, Jessica kissed her on the cheek and went on her way.

"Miss Nettle," Mrs. Bierce said as Jessica passed by her pew. "You and your sister are coming to our little get together this afternoon, are you not?"

Jessica stepped into the pew in front of the woman, out of the aisle. "We would not dream of missing it. Your Christmas Eve party is always one of my favorite events of the season."

Mrs. Bierce, a woman in her fifties with several children near Jessica's age, colored up. "Sweet girl. We certainly haven't the prestige of our marquess, but I do hope I give the young people something to look forward to." Mrs. Bierce limited her Christmas Eve party to people who were already out in Society and the young married couples in the neighborhood.

Every year they came together under her roof to play cards, sing carols, and then hurry away home before nightfall, when tradition held the spirits walked the cold roads and haunted the woods.

The matron turned to the aisle again, smiling in welcome as she said, "And you, Mr. Webb? We are always happy when you accompany Mr. Franklin Thackery to our afternoon of jolliness."

Though determined not to speak with Ellis, Jessica turned to see him blocking her in the pew. He bowed, his expression pleasant but unsmiling. "Of course, Mrs. Bierce. I would not miss it for the world."

"Delightful." Mrs. Bierce colored up again. Really, a woman of her age ought not to blush so easily. "We will expect everyone at two o'clock, and we will send you home before the sun sets." She glanced away from them to the rear of the church. "Oh, there is Mrs. Kincade. I must ensure her sons will attend. If you will both excuse me." She took her leave in a hurry, bustling down the aisle.

Jessica linked her hands together and stared at Ellis. He stared back, unmoving. Unsmiling. So she finally sighed and gestured to the aisle. "Will you step aside, sir? I need to join my family so we might leave."

His eyebrow slanted upward, and he looked over his shoulder to where her family stood, still in their pew, speaking to the Thackerys. Then he pointedly turned his attention back to her. "They do not seem to be in any hurry."

Drat. Jessica sighed and pushed a curl of hair behind her ear. She had tried to frame her face with several spirals, but her hair was too long for them to hold well. Not like Florence's curls that wound tightly around her forehead like a golden chain.

"Have you something particular you wish to say to me?" Sometimes, bluntness proved best.

"No." Then he held his arm out to her. "I would like to

escort you to your family's conveyance, if you will allow it."

"Why?" The word popped out on its own, tainted heavily with suspicion.

Rather than appear surprised, Ellis tipped his head to one side. His eyes lit with amusement. "Why not? It is a friendly enough thing to do."

She nearly reminded him that they were not friends. That they would never be friends. But she had already been rude enough. "Very well." She stepped closer and put her hand upon his forearm. He immediately took that hand and repositioned it, looping it around his arm and tucking it snuggly inside his elbow. Something about his rearrangement of her person felt strangely possessive. It made her cheeks flush with heat.

As he walked her slowly through the throng of her neighbors and friends, Jessica tried to ignore him and wish those around her a merry Christmas. But as people engaged them both in conversation, it became increasingly difficult to pretend she did not see the speculative stares directed at their joined arms. Drat the man again. He would make people suspect things they had no right to suspect.

Already, he made her far too aware of him. He smelled of citrus and cedar. His arm was strong. The heat of his body along her side made her want to draw near, especially as they came closer to the doors of the church where the winter air crept in. He spoke to everyone kindly, though his expression remained closed.

Jessica had spent years trying to hate Ellis, and yet mere minutes in his company seemed to be removing layer upon layer of her grudge. She had kept her distance to avoid that very thing. Their temporary truce was going to ruin everything. It would make her forget her anger and humiliation from years past. Resignedly, Jessica admitted to herself the greatest danger of all; all this time in Ellis's company would surely make her fall in love with him anew. And a woman's love would be so much different than a child's.

When they exited the church at last, fully surrounded by the chill, Jessica inhaled deeply, willing the cold in her lungs to spread to her heart. Except Ellis pulled her closer against his side, and he ducked his head to speak to her around the edge of her bonnet.

"Tighten your scarf, Miss Nettle. You cannot catch cold the day before Christmastide." He paused to let her do just that, then trapped her arm again.

Why did he have to be so thoughtful? Up until the moment he handed her into the first of her family's two sleighs, a driver alone waiting for them, she did not speak to him. Then she had to look into his eyes as she settled upon the bench. "Thank you, Mr. Webb."

"I will see you at the Bierce home in a short time." He bowed to her. "Until then, keep warm, Miss Nettle." And he strode away, as though the entire interaction between them was commonplace. The horrid, awful man. Did he not know, not suspect, how his presence worked upon her heart?

Jessica looked to the church doors and saw Florence on the arm of Franklin as he escorted her to the sleighs, but brothers surrounded them on all sides. Jessica scowled and turned her attention to her muff. She ought to have walked out with Florence, keeping Franklin from her sister as much as possible.

They could not be in love. And that was where she must keep her focus. Ellis Webb was less an ally and more a distraction to her purpose.

Or so she told herself, all the while thinking of his fine voice singing carols behind her during services.

CHAPTER 10

THE LAUGHTER AROUND CARD TABLES OUGHT TO HAVE lifted Jessica's mood. Instead, she forced herself to smile over the rim of her mug of chocolate. She had played several hands of Whist with her friends, then begged a moment to enjoy refreshments near the fire. The whole of the Bierces' home smelled of cinnamon, pine, and chocolate. Servants filled and refilled pots of peppermint tea and trays of biscuits. The large room in which everyone sat, talking and playing, was actually two rooms with connecting doors thrown open wide.

Though the fire crackled merrily nearby, and everyone around her spoke with anticipation of the Twelve Days of Christmas, Jessica's thoughts centered on her sister and Franklin. The two of them sat at a table together, partners in a game of Whist, which Florence played very well and Franklin very ill.

They did not suit each other. They had to see it. Florence excelled at nearly everything she tried, while Franklin bumbled through even the simplest conversations with her. What did Florence see in him? Did she seek the comfort of marrying a man who lived close to her family's home? Was it merely his sheepish smile and the curls atop his head which attracted her?

Jessica loved her sister, but she certainly did not understand her. If Jessica had her choice of men, she would not choose someone so quick to laugh at himself. She would much prefer someone who moved about the world with confidence and dignity. A man with a mind bent on learning and exploration. Not someone content to sit at home in his own library, with no need to see what more the world could offer.

Mrs. Bierce came through the room where the "young people," as she called them, sat and partook of refreshment rather than cards. "What a delight to have so many of you about," she proclaimed to the room at large. "I do wonder—is there anyone who would like to take up carols? The pianoforte is newly tuned, and I do so love music."

The gentlewomen of the neighborhood all exchanged glances and smiles, and two ladies sitting near Jessica stood at the same time and then laughed. They were sisters—one married, one not. Together they went to the instrument in the corner and began shuffling through the music laid out for the purpose.

Florence drifted into the room and spotted Jessica as the music began. Jessica waved her sister to sit beside her, which Florence did. Through the sound of the music, Jessica leaned in closer to her younger sister. "Here you are at last. I thought you meant to gamble away the family fortune with your playing."

"It was only pennies," Florence said with a wave of her

hand. "And Mr. Thackery saw to it that we lost as often as we won." She spoke with a fond smile rather than irritation. "You did not last long at cards today."

"No one came up to scratch as a partner." Jessica took another sip of her warm drink. "I play best when I play with you."

"Perhaps you ought to train someone new to sit across the table from you." Florence leaned in and spoke in a sly undertone. "Mr. Thackery thinks his cousin would make you a fine partner, you know."

Heat rushed from Jessica's chest up her neck and into her cheeks. "Why would he suggest such a thing? Everyone knows we detest one another." She tried to hide behind her cup again.

"I wonder at that." Florence smoothed her skirts, then clapped with everyone else as the first song came to a close. When the next began, she continued on a different subject entirely. "You and I ought to sing a duet."

"You are far more fond of public performance than I am." Jessica put her now-empty cup on a table near the couch. "The part written for alto singers is never as exciting as soprano. I am lucky if I sing over one note for the entirety of a song."

"*Greensleeves*," Florence suggested suddenly. "You are quite a natural at *Greensleeves*."

"Isn't that a bit solemn for a Christmas Eve party?" Jessica raised her eyebrows, but before Florence answered, Ellis entered the room. With Franklin. The two of them spotted the sisters at the same time, and Franklin led the way through the chairs and tables toward them. Jessica tipped her chin up. "I think it a better song for men's voices, too."

Franklin did not sing. Though it was something Florence took great joy in, Jessica knew he shrunk from it.

The men arrived, and Franklin sat next to Florence on the long couch. Ellis took a slender wood chair from the wall and moved it to sit at Jessica's arm.

Franklin grinned widely, ever and always amused with the world around him. "Ah, Miss Nettle. Did your sister tell you how hopelessly I lost all our pennies at Whist?"

"Indeed. I heard that news." Jessica arched an eyebrow at him, leaning forward just enough to peer around her sister at him. She ignored Ellis steadfastly, despite his nearness. "But when you came upon us, we were discussing taking a turn in song. Florence is fond of the oldest carols. She suggested *Greensleeves.* What do you think of that one, Mr. Thackery? Is it not too solemn for the afternoon?"

Eager as he was to please Florence, as Jessica suspected, Franklin hurried to agree. "I enjoy that song immensely. It is among my favorites of the season. One can imagine the romance that inspired such lyrics must have been heartfelt." He grinned widely. "I can think of nothing so enjoyable as hearing a talented singer bring life to the old tune."

He fell so easily into her trap, Jessica thought it almost unsporting. Yet she smiled broadly at him. "Delightful. Then you will sing it for us?"

His smile melted away. "Me?" His face paled.

"Yes. A gentleman's voice does better credit to the lyrics. I do so long to hear it. As does Florence. Is that not so, Sister? It is one of your favorites, is it not?"

Florence watched Franklin as intently as Jessica, though her expression was one of concern rather than glee. "It is my favorite, but we need not impose on Mr. Thackery—"

"Nonsense. It cannot be an imposition when he declared the song one of his favorites, too. Come. I will play for you." The song played by the two sisters was coming to an end, and Jessica had to move quickly before someone else inserted themselves at the instrument. "Do come." She did not look behind her as she made her way to the instrument. He would join her and muddle his way through the song, or he would not, and make her appear foolish in front of her sister and everyone else.

It was a good test of his affection for Florence. If a man was not willing to look foolish, or at least attempt to please a woman with so simple a thing, then his could not be a true love. At least, she reasoned that a momentary sacrifice of public display would be but a little thing to a man in love.

As she neared the pianoforte, she smiled warmly at the musicians as they took in the applause. They made eye contact, and the sisters happily departed the instrument to allow Jessica to take up the chair at the ivory and ebony keys. She squared her shoulders, held her hands at the ready, and looked up for the first time to see if Franklin had followed or stayed behind.

And she met the formidable stare belonging to Ellis Webb. Franklin remained next to Jessica, she saw, when she darted a glance back to the couch, and it was Ellis coming to stand beside her. She swallowed.

Ellis cocked his head to the side, and then he maneuvered so he stood where she could see him as she played. Surely, he did not mean to sing with her? As they stared at one another, her hands hanging in the air, the room quieted. Her chest tightened.

No. He could not sing with her. Not this song. Looking at her. Did he not remember the lyrics? This was a love song. Not a Christmas carol in any traditional sense. That people sang it at Christmastide had always perplexed her, no matter that she loved the song as much as her sister. Perhaps more.

Someone coughed in the quiet, and a woman tittered. Jessica's silent stare had turned the two of them into a spectacle. And it was Ellis who saved them.

"We did not mean to take attention away from the party, but we hope our friends will help settle a matter of debate for us." He kept his solemn expression, his deep voice carrying through one room and into the other, attracting the attention of those who had not yet noticed their strange display at the pianoforte. "We will perform *Greensleeves* but put it to each of you to decide if it is a song appropriate for Christmas celebrations or if it is too solemn for a company such as ours." Then he nodded to Jessica, as though she had been waiting for his signal all along.

She tried to relax her hands as she pressed her fingers to the keys and played an introduction to the melody. The song was ancient, well-known throughout England, though none knew its origins. Some said King Henry VIII wrote it for the ill-fated Anne Boleyn, others said it harkened back to the time of Chaucer. Whatever the genuine history, every child knew the lyrics and Jessica could play the arrangement on the pianoforte from memory.

When the time came for Ellis's voice to join the music,

the richness of his tone permeated every particle of air and made the room tremble. Melancholy as the lyrics were, his voice turned them into something heart-achingly beautiful. Her fingers played the keys by memory alone, as she closed her eyes to listen with her whole being. She had heard Ellis sing before. Many times. When his voice deepened from boyish tones to the elegance of a man grown, she had fallen more in love with him.

But she had never heard him like this.

He sung as though he had written the words himself, so earnest he sounded. And her heart trembled. As he sang the chorus for the final time, Jessica opened her eyes to look at him—and she stopped playing. She could not possibly touch the keys again, but he continued singing without her accompaniment. She could not play because he stared at her, as though singing *to* her.

Greensleeves was my delight,
Greensleeves my heart of gold
Greensleeves was my heart of joy
And who but my lady Greensleeves?

The quiet lingered for one long second, and then there was applause. Applause and enthusiastic exclamations from around the room, though she could not focus to hear what was said. Instead, she stared at Ellis, as confused and heartsore as she had been the Christmas day he had refused to bestow a kiss upon her. Again, she felt small and foolish. Again, her heart burst with unrequited love.

Despite everything she had told herself over the years, and all the horrid things she had done to him to sow discord and create distance between them, all that had vanished with one song. One look.

Ellis's eyebrows pulled sharply together, and she saw

the puzzlement in his expression. He did not have even an iota of understanding. Jessica remained alone in her feelings. As she always would.

She stood from the pianoforte, and when he took a step toward her, she turned around and fled. No one noticed. The conversations had resumed. The players at the card tables were already laughing again. But she twisted her way through everyone to the doorway, and then out into the corridor where only servants came and went. She hurried down the staircase to the ground floor of the house. Away from everyone. Needing to compose herself. Her defenses had fallen, and nothing could be more disastrous.

Ellis attempted to go after Jessica. The distress he had seen in her eyes had made him want nothing more than to charge to her side, to protect her from whatever had hurt her. But he did not make it across the room before Florence stepped into his path. She wore a broad smile that did not reach her eyes.

"Oh, Mr. Webb, that was wonderful. An excellent performance."

Jessica disappeared into the corridor. He needed to follow.

"Thank you. If you will excuse me—"

Florence's hand was suddenly upon his wrist, gently squeezing. He looked down at her in surprise. She offered him the slightest shake of her head. "Won't you come to the refreshment table with me? You must try this delightful cake. Lemon, I think it is."

He frowned down at her, realizing immediately that Florence was purposefully keeping him from going after Jessica. Though why she would do such a thing, he could not understand. But he trusted her. "Of course. Please. Lead the way."

She wove through the other guests to a refreshment table near the windows, but she did not stop there. She walked to the corner of the room where Franklin joined them. Then Florence, false cheer still upon her face, spoke quietly and with speed. "You absolutely may not go after Jessica. She will not thank you for it, and others may misconstrue your relationship with her."

Franklin tucked his hands behind his back. "Quite right, Ellis. Give her a moment to compose herself."

Looking between them, Ellis slowly agreed. "Very well. Though why you are not more concerned with her, I cannot understand."

Florence looked to Franklin, who exchanged a mysteriously sad expression with her. Then the young woman addressed Ellis again. "It is you who do not understand, Mr. Webb. But it is not up to me to explain things to you. Please, trust me. Jessica is best left alone for now. I will attend to her in a moment."

"Come with me, Cousin." Franklin pointed to another doorway that would take them to the billiard room. "Let us find entertainment elsewhere for a time."

Ellis allowed himself to be led away and then spent a quarter of an hour watching Franklin play poorly at billiards. When he'd had enough of that, he made his way back into the sitting room. Other ladies played the pianoforte and sang a wassailing song from generations past.

Jessica and Florence sat in the other room at a card table, partners in a game. Jessica seemed to have composed herself, though her smile appeared dampened and uncertain. When Florence laughed, Jessica did not.

Something strange had happened while he sang. He had only meant to save Franklin embarrassment. Franklin, despite many a valiant effort at song, had no ear for music. He frequently missed notes or sang the wrong one altogether. When Jessica had insisted he join her, had nearly made a fool of Franklin, Ellis had nearly lost his temper with her. She had known the Thackery family since infancy. She had to be aware of Franklin's situation. Yet she had pressured him anyway. Ellis knew she had done so on purpose, and he had stepped in.

But his insertion into the situation had changed it. While he had certainly saved Franklin, he had somehow wounded Jessica. He watched her from the doorway, puzzling things out. Was it the music? His voice? Merely that he had thwarted her plans that upset her?

Jessica hadn't been angry. She had appeared hurt and lost. And it was somehow his doing.

Ellis did not approach her again that afternoon. Not even when everyone lined up in the entry hall to take their leave. He stayed well back, though Franklin went to Florence to bid her good afternoon.

As he and Franklin rode home, their horses high-stepping through the snow, Ellis turned his mind to the next time his path must cross with Jessica's.

He would see her on the morrow. Christmas Day meant a gathering at the Nettle home in the evening, after dinner. The family hosted evening tea and an informal evening of dancing and merriment for many of their neighbors. They invited as many as they could to stay up most of the night and use good cheer to chase away old superstitions. Ellis had always enjoyed those evenings.

Franklin hummed to himself as they left the main road for the path that would take them to Lamblyn Court, as off-key as ever, but happier than Ellis had ever seen him.

"You are abominably cheerful," Ellis muttered aloud.

His cousin laughed. "I cannot help it. I grow happier every time I am in Miss Florence's company."

"Even though her sister was distressed?" Ellis hadn't exactly meant to ask the question. It had fallen from his lips without his permission.

"Even then." Franklin's grin did not diminish. "Miss Nettle will recover from whatever shock she suffered today, and tomorrow I will see my beloved. Perhaps I will even be so fortunate as to catch her beneath the mistletoe."

Ellis shook his head, releasing a puff of exasperated air. "She told you where it's hidden, didn't she?"

"Perhaps." His grin turned impudent. "And I will certainly take advantage of that knowledge, as she wishes me to do." He released a joyful laugh. "I am in love with Florence, and I intend to ask for her hand come the New Year."

"Congratulations." Ellis said the single word automatically, though he sighed directly after. "I suppose that means you will be even more insufferably cheerful than normal."

"Absolutely." Franklin's cheer made even his horse perk up, ears forward and head coming up. "I will torture you with my happiness until you are wise enough to seek your own."

"Why is it that married people—or those who consider themselves as good as wed—are always forcing the same state onto their friends?" Ellis dropped his head to avoid a low branch covered in icicles. "Leave us alone in our happily single state."

"You have no idea what you are missing," Franklin argued cheerfully. "To fall in love is an adventure. It is both ecstasy and sublime agony, not knowing if your affection is returned. Then, when you can see that the lady who holds your heart does so with tenderness of feeling—"

"Enough," Ellis said, pleading. "I want no more descriptions of your feelings or hers. Should you even speak so freely of them when you are not yet attached?" He glowered at his friend, who appeared completely unrepentant. "Frank. Spare me, please."

"You are disappointingly dull." Franklin sat straighter on his mount. "Shall we race the rest of the way? That may bring your spirits up."

"If it will stop your rhapsodizing about Miss Florence, I will race to Scotland and back." Ellis did not wait for his friend to call the start but urged his horse into a canter and then a gallop. His cousin laughed behind them, and soon their mounts pounded up the lane to Lamblyn Court, the subject of hearts and marriage left behind them in the snow.

Christmas Eve in the Thackery home had always been subdued. They came together for a family meal, lit a Yule Candle, then stayed awake together until near dawn. The boys played games, then they read aloud from books containing old ghost stories until the darkness outside turned to light. At dawn, each man and boy lumbered up the stairs to seek their bed until much later in the day.

Franklin had told Ellis, years and years before, that they had started staying up late when their mother had died. Mr. Thackery missed his late wife, and his grief came heavily at Christmas. His sons wanted to offer comfort, and Franklin had given them the idea to keep their father company on the long night. Though the woman he mourned was Franklin's stepmother, he treated his father's feelings with kindness.

So it was after midnight that Ellis sat in the study, and he stared silently into the fire. The three young Thackery lads played a game with their father at the table, and Franklin dozed quietly in a chair nearby, a book in his hand.

Ellis thought of Jessica, the way she had been when she played the pianoforte for him. He had watched her close her eyes, her fingers still dancing across the keys while her expression turned fervent. All because it was him who sang rather than Franklin. While he had volunteered to sing in Franklin's place, thinking to thwart her plan, it had only taken a few moments of the song for his heart to turn over in a way that made the world shift.

A log in the fireplace popped and fell, bringing him from his thoughts. Ellis rose and used the fire poker to rearrange the logs before adding another. And there, kneeling by the fire, he thought again on the moment when Jessica's eyes had opened during the final lines of the chorus.

Her blue-green gaze had collided with his, full of an emotion he did not understand. Pain. Surprise. A mix of things both alarming and confusing. That her first instinct had been to run from him made him contemplate that moment. Because his first thought had been the opposite —he had wanted nothing more than to go to her and offer comfort.

He suddenly doubted that a return to their former friendship would be enough for him. He admired her, yes. He'd been willing to admit that much. But what if that admiration had turned to something more?

CHAPTER 11

Jessica loved Christmas day. No matter what came the rest of the year, the magic of a day filled with family, friends, and merriment held a place in her heart she would never relinquish. She laid in bed that morning, staring up at the ceiling, thinking only on what the day would bring.

Every Christmas, the family rose late and ate breakfast together, bursting with happiness and excitement. After breakfast, the Nettle children always received a gift from their parents to mark the day. They spent the day together in the library, playing snapdragon and all manner of ridiculous games. Then they would attend Evensong at the church before dinner and the family party.

This morning, as she stayed snug in her bed a few extra moments, Jessica had to fight away the thoughts that threatened to ruin her day. She refused to think about Ellis Webb and his beautiful voice as he sang the day before. The knowledge that he would attend their Christmas party that evening did not cause her heart even the slightest flutter. Yet, the longer she stayed abed, the more she had to convince her mind to stop wandering his direction.

With a huff, Jessica threw off her blankets and put both feet on the floor. She shivered once, then went to the fire already blazing thanks to an industrious maid. After summoning help to dress, Jessica left her room with head held high and a Christmas spring in her step. Before long, the entire household was awake and alive with laughter. Her family sat around the breakfast table, Aunt Temperance included, discussing the day ahead.

After a sumptuous breakfast feast, Mother, Father, Aunt Temperance, Jessica, Florence, Robert, Henry, and Matthew crowded into the morning room. The Nettles spent many winter hours in the room, as its window faced south and had more enjoyment of the winter sun than most of the other sitting rooms.

"Now then," Papa said, standing before the hearth. "Our gifts to each of you this year are of a practical nature. We hope you will not find them wanting." And thus the exchange of presents began.

From her parents, Jessica received a pair of ruby earrings with a matching bracelet. Florence gifted her an ebony inked box to keep her jewelry stored prettily. Robert handed her a book. Henry, a skein of red ribbon. And Matthew, too young to be practical, gave her sweets purchased from the apothecary with his pocket money. Jessica returned their gifts with small tokens of her own, each item created in her careful way. At last, she sat at Aunt Temperance's feet.

Her aunt rested in a large chair with gold-gilded arms

and a soft green cushion for a seat. Mutton hid beneath the chair, watching the festivities with suspicion.

"Aunt Tempie, this is for you." Jessica presented her great aunt with a small, oval portrait of Mutton. She had captured the dog's curious tilt of the head and shining black eyes with great care and had fitted it into the oval frame chosen especially for her aunt's gift.

"Oh, Jessica. How lovely." Aunt Temperance held the dog's portrait and laughed. "It is his very image! This rascal of a dog means the world to me. Thank you, my dear. I will treasure this miniature for the rest of my days." She held the oval frame to her heart, and Jessica beamed up at her aunt. The gift had felt right, though Florence had thought it sounded silly. Aunt Temperance's enthusiasm proved it perfect.

"I am delighted you like it." Jessica turned to watch her family, the warmth of their love filling her heart and soul.

A touch upon Jessica's shoulder made her look up. She saw a thoughtful gleam in Aunt Temperance's eyes. "I have something for you, too." Aunt Temperance had already distributed gifts. Sheets of music from faraway lands for the young ladies, wine from France for her father, Irish lace for her mother, and elaborate penknives from her late-husband's collection to the boys.

Her aunt produced a small parcel from the reticule on her wrist and handed it to Jessica. "My husband gave it to me to mark the first year of our marriage. I think it is time I pass it on to you." Her lips pursed, and she spoke with lightness. "You do so remind me of myself, at times."

"That is a high compliment," Jessica declared, though she suspected her aunt meant more than that. She slipped the piece of twine off the package and unfolded the brown paper, the slight weight of the object making her curious.

Two slender pieces of polished wood, carved with images of roses, rested in her palm. She noted a hinge in the wood and lifted the opposite edge upward to reveal a compass. It was a beautiful piece, inlaid with silver, and the arrow trembled as she turned it in her hands. It pointed north.

Tears stung her eyes. "Thank you, Aunt Temperance." It was beautiful.

"I hope you will take it with you on all your adventures," her aunt said gently. "It has always guided me true."

Jessica shook her head and closed the compass. "I am uncertain I should accept this, then. I will likely never go farther away from home than the next county." She tried to laugh at the fact but could summon no true playfulness. Instead, her voice only sounded wavering and sad, even to her ears.

"Dear girl. You are young. There is time." Aunt Temperance produced a handkerchief from her bosom and dabbed at the tears escaping Jessica's eyes. "Besides, as I said, you are like me. Once you determine what your heart wants, nothing will stand in your way. I am certain of it."

Before Jessica could respond, Mutton darted out from the chair, barking wildly and charging at Matthew. The boy had found a lion mask amid his gifts and put it on, and the little dog seemed to think the beast there to challenge him and him alone. The family laughed while Matthew growled and chased Mutton around the room, only for Mutton to dart beneath a chair and come up behind Matthew, chomping on the boy's coat.

Conversation began anew, and Jessica sat quietly with her compass in hand. She opened it again and went to the southward facing windows. Standing there, facing outward, the needle of the compass pointed squarely at Jessica's heart.

Her aunt's words drifted to the forefront of her mind.

What did Jessica want? Travel, of course. Adventure. But there was more. She wanted so much more.

The ride to the Thackery home late that evening necessitated that lanterns hang on the sleighs and carriages that made their way along the roads. Ellis sat next to Franklin, who drove his family's sleigh with merriment that seemed indecent, given the low temperatures and threat of yet more snow in the air. Even with hot bricks at their feet, robes upon their laps, and all their winter clothing, Ellis fought to keep from shivering.

The boys talked excitedly behind him, and Mr. Thackery's deep voice answered them from time to time.

No one noticed when Franklin asked, "Did you bring a gift for Miss Nettle?"

Ellis peered over the edge of the scarf he had wrapped around him from neck to nose. "Absolutely not. Don't be ridiculous."

Franklin had the audacity to look at Ellis as though he were the one proposing odd things. "It is Christmas. And you want to be in her good graces, do you not?"

"No. Whatever gave you that idea?" Ellis faced forward again. He had no intention of making Jessica uncomfortable by giving her a gift she surely didn't desire. Although he did have his own plans for restoring himself in her eyes. He meant to offer her every opportunity to see that he would be a far better friend than an enemy. And, perhaps, something more than friendship might bloom. In time.

His was of a practical nature. At least, he told himself that several times over. And practical men did not suddenly bestow gifts upon women where they had never given gifts before.

They arrived at Brookfield House at the same moment as several other neighbors. The doors were flung open wide, despite the chill in the air, as guests poured inside the warmth of the stately home. After handing the sleigh and horses off to a groom, the Thackerys made their way up the stairs. Ellis followed behind, looking through the crowd to try to find Jessica in the throng.

He found the bright hair of her sister first, reflecting the lantern light in an angelic halo. Franklin made his way that direction, but Ellis remained near the door a moment. When he still could not find Jessica, he started up the stairs to the upstairs rooms where the party took place. His eyes skimmed across the crowd below, but he still did not see her.

He went up to the rail and leaned over it, finding every member of Jessica's family except for the woman herself. Where might she be? Surely she attended the party in her home. She would not hide away from him. Had he misstepped so horribly on Christmas Eve that she now avoided Ellis altogether?

"Are you looking for something?" a voice asked at his

elbow, and he turned his head in some surprise to see that Jessica had materialized at his side. She leaned against the rail, looking down into the crowd with him. "I suppose this is the best vantage point in the house." She glanced sideways at him, and her lips turned upward in a gentle smile.

His mouth went dry as his eyes drank her in. Her honey-colored hair glowed like a flickering fire. Those fairy-ring eyes danced with the joy of the season and her usual mischief. Rubies glinted at her ears and around her throat, matching her gown of red. A gown which fit her feminine form perfectly. Roses bloomed in her cheeks, defying the wintry weather with their joyous color.

"You are lovely this evening, Miss Nettle." He did not mean to compliment her. Such words had only seemed to make her suspicious of him. As though he'd been the one playing tricks all these years rather than her.

Jessica smirked and looked away. "You are too kind, and most insincere. But I thank you for the play to my vanity."

Her remark stung. Ellis corrected his posture, prepared to offer up proof of his sincerity. But the bark of a little dog stopped him, and he looked down to see Mutton staring at him from the carpet. The dog wagged its tail and yipped again.

"Oh, there you are." Mrs. Bolingbrooke came out of a doorway, dressed in green velvet and wearing black ostrich feathers in her hair. "I beg your pardon, Mr. Webb. It seems that Mutton has taken a liking to you."

"I cannot think why." Despite his solemn tone, he bent down to give the dog attention. The distraction of the animal helped him put his foolish heart in place.

"Nor can I," Jessica added, still standing above him. "He is normally such a sensible dog."

Ellis had to duck his head to hide a grin, but Mrs. Bolingbrooke laughed. Then she said, "Come now. Mutton is an excellent judge of character. He must sense good things about you, Mr. Webb. But for now, my little dog must go to the nursery. He certainly cannot stay here and be a nuisance to the guests."

"I can take him for you, Aunt Tempie." Jessica bent and scooped up the dog, and for a moment Ellis's gaze collided with hers. How beautiful she was, and how much he wished he could tell her and be believed. But she left in an instant, leaving Ellis to stand at the landing with Mrs. Bolingbrooke.

"My Jess is a lovely woman, is she not?" the matron asked, drawing his attention back to her. Though she was old enough to be his grandmother, the woman had a sprightly air about her. Perhaps because of how she held herself, or maybe it was the near-match in color of her eyes to Jessica's, but she did not seem *old*. Especially when her gaze turned calculating.

"I agree with you, madam." He then gestured to the crowd below as laughter and conversation drifted upward. "And she is certainly among the best company here."

"Why is it that you agree with me?" The woman's chin tilted down as she peered up at him.

He had always appreciated Jessica's wit. But he chose a different answer for her great-aunt. "Because she has a gift for setting people at ease, whether it is with conversation or comfortable silence. A talent that many lack, and therefore makes her delightful in company."

"A charming answer." Mrs. Bolingbrooke nodded to

the open doors along the corridor. "Escort me to the gallery, young man, before everyone else comes stampeding up the stairs when they realize where they ought to be."

With a chuckle, he offered his arm to the older woman. She put an ivory-gloved hand near his wrist and walked with the stateliness of a queen. "I have studied you since we first met, you know."

"Have you?" Ellis did not bother hiding his smile. "I cannot imagine what interest I hold as a specimen."

"You are too modest, sir. I suspect you know exactly why I find you of interest. Your cousin is enamored with my Florence. But you, I think, are newly aware that women exist as more than mere ornamentation."

Ellis chuckled dryly. Her tone told him there was no purpose in refuting her words. Even if he wanted to. Instead, he played along with her conversation. "My mother would turn me out of her house if she suspected I viewed women thus. As her only child, she took great pleasure in instilling within me a respect for the meeker sex. I am a man who recognizes the intelligence and importance of the women in his life. I promise."

"Still." Mrs. Bolingbrooke arched her graying eyebrows at him, then nodded to the chair on the far side of the room she wished to take. "I would wager my feathers on the fact that you have given no thought to securing a member of the 'meeker sex' to you through more than acquaintance until recently."

She had him there. Given her sly smile, she knew it, too. Clever woman. No wonder he liked her. It seemed she had a touch of Jessica's sly nature.

"If that is true, madam, what does it signify to you?"

He released her arm as she lowered herself into a green-and-gold chair. The long gallery held chairs and benches aplenty, as well as works of art and portraits of Thackery ancestors along its walls. The long hall was perfect for large parties and doubled easily as a ballroom.

"It signifies, along with my observations, that you might have designed a plan for the conquering of my great-niece's heart. Given Jessica's response to you this evening, I think you may be in need of guidance, if that is the case."

Here at last, he paused and some of his amusement left him. "The same sort of guidance you offered Miss Florence, perhaps?"

"Similar. As much as you young people like to think yourselves independent and capable of conquering the world, sometimes a more experienced mind is useful." She leaned back in her chair, appearing as relaxed as a monarch upon her thrown. "Think on it, young man."

He bowed but made no promises as he took his leave. Having a person—even someone as well-meaning as Mrs. Bolingbrooke—interfere with his life did not sit well with him. The unsettled feeling that idea caused had goaded Jessica into action, too.

Why did anyone set themselves up as matchmakers? Playing with people's hearts and lives could cause pain as often as it caused pleasure. Poor Franklin had become a complete fool in his hopes for love, and Miss Florence could likely snap her fingers and command him.

People streamed into the gallery. Including Franklin, with Miss Florence on his arm. The poor man stared at her as though the house could fall around his ears, and he would not even take notice.

Love ought to be more sensible than that. If two people came together naturally and had an affection for one another, that was all there was to it. Like his parents. They were steady in their feelings. Their love was mature, and he could not imagine it being any other way.

He approached the idea of caring for Jessica as rationally as possible. He remained calm. Yes, he had admired her beauty only a moment ago, to the point that he found it difficult to speak. But it was only because that was his first glimpse of her, arrayed as she was in her Christmas finery.

"Mr. Webb, here you are."

His heart stuttered within his chest as he turned on his heel to find that Jessica had sneaked up behind him again. Her usual crooked smile appeared, and Ellis amended his thoughts. Something had changed within him, because seeing Jessica altered the state of his being. He bowed to her. "Here I am. Have you need of me, Miss Nettle?"

"No."

Her answer deflated him at once. "Ah. Well. If there is anything I might do for you—" He broke off his polite offer upon seeing the glittering mirth in her eyes. He glowered at her. "You must think yourself quite amusing."

"Of course I do. People find me delightful."

As he had used that very word to describe her moments before, he could not argue that point. Why did he want to argue with her at all? "So there *is* something you want from me?" he asked, all solemnity once again.

"Yes, there is. I would like you to help me keep Mr. Thackery and my sister from standing together in the

northwest corner of the room." She tilted her head to indi-
cate the direction where his eyes darted with interest.

"Why? What is in that corner?"

"I have it on good authority that my sister placed a
kissing bough in the greenery hanging above my great-
grandfather's portrait. He is a solemn-faced gentleman
dressed in a coat the color of periwinkles."

"Can we consider a gentleman solemn if he wears
such a shade?" Ellis adjusted the cuffs of his more sensible
deep blue evening coat.

"It was the mid-eighteenth century, Mr. Webb. Men
dressed as peacocks, whereas now they only act the part
with their arrogant posturing." She batted her eyelashes
at him meaningfully. "Keep your cousin away from that
corner, unless you want his affection for my sister on
display for everyone to speculate about."

She took a step away, but Ellis caught her arm gently
to stop her. "Would you honor me with a dance this
evening?" Blast and hang it all. He hadn't meant to sound
so eager. He released her and tucked the offending hand
behind his back. "In the spirit of Christmas."

Jessica's cheeks turned pink. She stepped closer, her
voice lowered. "It never fails to astound me how cavalier
men are when they ask a woman to dance. Knowing as
they do that should she wish to refuse him, she may not
stand up with any gentleman for the whole of the
evening."

"Oh." He had imagined her blush, then. And everything else that made him think they had a chance to
rekindle a less antagonistic relationship. His cheeks
burned with humiliation. "I have no wish to make you
uncomfortable, or to force my company on you. Pretend I

never asked." He bowed, but midway through the motion, she said his name. Not his surname. His Christian name.

"Ellis, no. Stop." She held her hand out, and he followed the trail of her gloved palm up her arm, shoulder, graceful neck, and to those bewitching eyes. They were wide, and her expression distraught. "I am sorry. My tongue ran away from me. Please forgive me."

He hesitated, warily returning to his stiff posture. "There is nothing to forgive, except my assumption that a truce might also mean a dance." He smiled, but he felt the unpleasant tightness in the gesture.

"I do want to dance with you," she said, her voice low. Her gaze darted away, and color stole into her cheeks again. "It is only that I cannot think why you would ask me, especially now. I have been so terrible. Your invitation surprised me, and I said the first thing that came to my mind. Because it is frustrating." Her gaze came back to his, the earnest tone giving him more reason to believe her. "I cannot tell you how many times an unpleasant gentleman has asked me to dance, and if I want to enjoy myself at all, I have to stand up with him or else forfeit all partners of an evening. It is decidedly unfair, isn't it?"

"I had never stopped to consider the situation," he admitted as he tried not to smile. His offer had surprised her. To the point that she had blurted out a dearly held opinion rather than an honest answer. That had to be... good? It could not be a bad sign, surely. "One would think a man would be cognizant enough of a young lady's feelings to avoid making her anxious of such things."

"I suppose the best of gentlemen consider such things." He took in the way she relaxed, her hands at her sides and her shoulders dropping to a more comfortable height. Then she lowered her gaze to the floor between them. "Is your invitation still open, Mr. Webb?"

"Only if you call me Ellis." Perhaps his suggestion was too bold. But he had flustered her already, and found he enjoyed the blush in her cheeks and how she blurted out whatever was first on her mind. Perhaps he would gain more insight into Jessica's thoughts with such brazen words.

Her chin came up, and her eyes turned round and wide. The color in her cheeks deepened. "You are holding the dance hostage?" she asked, shock upon her features. "And am I to allow you the same liberty? Will you call me Jessica?"

He shrugged one shoulder, then adjusted the line of his coat. "If that is your wish."

Her mouth opened and closed again. Then she looked behind him and her eyebrows raised. "Very well, Ellis. You may have one dance. Now, stop distracting me. I need to look after my sister and Mr. Thackery." She stepped around him, and he let her go. Holding in a grin, Ellis walked in the opposite direction to the corner of the room infected by mistletoe.

Jessica kept close to her sister during most of the party. Ellis stayed along the wall where Florence had hidden her kissing bough, and that kept Jessica from making any more ridiculous conversation with him. Or revealing conversation. How foolish had she sounded, questioning an age-old facet of their society? And why, *why* had she agreed to call Ellis by his Christian name?

She meant to forget her feelings for him. To push them deep down into the darkest recesses of her heart. There they had languished for nearly seven years while she found every possible way to make him realize how much she did not like him.

The crusade had started the year she turned fifteen. The summer after he did not kiss her. When he was more boy than man, but still so far ahead of her when it came to everything. He grew farther away each time he went on an adventure, experiencing more of the world than she ever would. Growing too experienced and sophisticated for her, a little nobody who remained at home. Never traveling more than fifteen or twenty miles away from her home.

"You have been awfully quiet this evening." Florence led Jessica to the punch bowl. "You did not play snapdragon with our brothers, nor have you sat down at a card table even once. Instead, you have followed me around like a duckling."

Jessica picked up a cup and spoke as delicately as she held its handle. "I protest being likened to a flat-footed waterfowl."

"I notice you deny nothing else in my statement. What is it that has distracted you so?" Florence sipped at her punch, but her eyes were not on Jessica. It was a simple matter to follow her gaze to where Franklin stood amid a group of men. The two of them had stayed apart most of the evening. Perhaps they grew less enamored of each other already?

"I might ask you the same."

Neither had made any attempt to stand beneath the frightfully obvious mistletoe. Though other couples had certainly made use of the excuse to exchange a kiss in the open. Married couples. A few of their courting neighbors. But not Florence or Franklin. And Ellis remained standing guard, stoic as a soldier, making conversation with anyone who drifted near him.

Jessica noted the musicians taking their place in a recessed portion of the room near a large window. "Are you dancing this evening?"

A secretive smile stole across Florence's face. "What would Christmas be without dancing?" She drank her punch, then put her cup down on a tray. "And you? Will you dance?"

Jessica let her gaze drift to where Ellis had lingered, and despite the distance between them, their gazes found one another. Her heart fluttered hopefully, and Jessica reminded herself to stay calm. Reluctant though she was to follow her own advice. How much might she enjoy the evening if she let herself forget, for the space of a single dance, the years since that hurtful Christmas? If she pretended it had never happened, and she met Ellis as a near-stranger rather than an old friend?

He walked toward her as the musicians set about fine-tuning their instruments. Her parents made an announcement she barely heard—the same one they made every year, preparing to lead out the dance. It was the only time her father danced with her mother outside of their family practices. They looked forward to it all year.

Everything slipped from her mind when Ellis reached her and bowed. "I believe this is our dance, Miss Nettle." He held a gloved hand out to her as he lifted his head, and something quite different displaced his usual stoic expression. Something hopeful.

As Jessica slid her fingers into his warm grasp, her pulse loud in her ears, she did not pretend he was a mysterious stranger come to dance with her for a single evening. Rather, she let him return to a place of affection in her mind and heart. The place he had always belonged, if she only would have found a way to show it to him before.

The end of the gallery opposite where the infamous mistletoe lay was where everything had been cleared for those who wished to dance. Ellis led Jessica to their place in line, then released her hand as he took his place across from her. The music began, and they took their first steps toward each other.

Their dance was not one of great fashion or pomp. It was joyous, requiring quick steps and filled with bright laughter. Yet every time Jessica met Ellis's gaze, or her hand grasped his, she wanted nothing more than to let the music sweep them away. Away from every worry, disagreement, and her petty pranks.

Ellis had only asked her for a single dance. Not a set. So when the music ended, he took her by the hand again to escort her from the new lines. He walked with her to stand near one of the windows, where cool air seeped through the glass. He held her hand a moment longer than necessary, and she felt him squeeze her fingers as though reluctant to let her go.

"Ellis."

His eyes brightened. "Jessica."

She had so much to say to him. She wanted to apologize and begin again. But what if he asked why she had treated him so awfully before? She could not tell him of her childhood love. Not now. Not since it had blossomed into something so much deeper. Which would mean a greater hurt when he laughed at her and walked away.

Her great-aunt's arrival at their window saved Jessica from making a complete fool of herself.

"You two dance very well together." Aunt Temperance waved her black-feathered fan rapidly, then snapped it closed to tap Ellis on the arm. "I do not think I have had the pleasure of seeing you smile until this evening, young man. I find I must recommend you exercise that ability more, as it makes you appear most handsome. Far better than glowering. Do you not think so, Jessica?"

Ellis's smile had faded, but amusement twinkled in his eyes. "Your great-niece has no opinion about my smiles or frowns, Mrs. Bolingbrooke. Of that I assure you."

"Stuff and nonsense. If a woman of my advanced age notices a handsome gentleman when he smiles, you can be certain every woman of eligible age notices, too." She flicked her fan open again and turned to Jessica pointedly. Mortified as she was by her great-aunt's pronouncement, Jessica tried to laugh the discomfort away.

"Aunt Tempie, you cannot go about complimenting bachelors. It isn't done."

"It is if I do it," her aunt said stubbornly. "But that is neither here nor there. Come. I have need of you. Oh, and Mr. Webb, will you be so kind as to bring refreshment to my niece and myself? This way, Jessica."

Her aunt brooked no argument, so Jessica allowed herself to be herded across the room. She looked over her shoulder once to exchange a helpless look with Ellis, who shook his head and went to the table with all the punch cups.

"You cannot order him around like that, Aunt Tempie.

Mr. Webb is a gentleman, not a page boy." Although it had been somewhat amusing.

"When you are my age, dear girl, you order anyone younger than you to do your bidding. You will find very few argue." She stopped them both before a large globe that normally set in the middle of the gallery, as much a work of art as a functioning map. The globe's circumference was too large for Jessica to wrap her arms all the way around it, and the stand that held the green and gold sphere was carved intricately with flowering vines.

Ellis joined them, holding two cups of punch. "As you requested, Mrs. Bolingbrooke."

"Thank you." She took her cup while Jessica did the same, casting Ellis an apologetic glance. Then she looked to where the dangerous mistletoe waited for her sister and Mr. Franklin. She relaxed immediately when she saw neither of them near it. But where had they gone?

"Is there anything else I might do for you, madam?"

"Yes." Aunt Temperance nodded to the globe. "Show me exactly where you went when you visited Greece. I should like to know your route. Did you make most of the journey by sea, or by land? I always preferred land. More to take in that way."

Jessica turned her full attention to the globe, watching as Ellis let his finger hover above England and trace a path into Europe. He spoke in even tones about his adventure, and Jessica's throat tightened painfully as he described things he had seen. The blue of the water, the color of the birds, the heat of summer upon the sea.

Her eyes lingered on coastlines, tracing familiar shapes that would only ever be lines on a map to her.

Someone called her aunt's name, and Jessica was

dimly aware of her aunt excusing herself. She pulled in a deep breath, alarmed at the way her chest tightened. She looked up at Ellis, who had stayed beside her, to find him studying her rather than the globe.

"Does the idea of travel distress you?" he asked. "I thought your sister said you were eager to see the world."

Having been mocked for that desire too many times to count, Jessica laughed dismissively. "Eager?" Her heart longed for it. "I am certain Florence never said such a thing." She looked at the continent of Africa, and she let her eyes trace the coast of Spain.

"But do you wish to travel?" Ellis asked, leaning a little toward her as he spoke.

She lifted her face to his, searching his eyes. Would he mock her? Or pity her? Perhaps neither. Ellis had always been patient. Except when she pushed him too far with her jests. Then he was quick to speak, to say things that penetrated her mind and made her withdraw in guilt.

"Sometimes, I think I would like to," she admitted, almost too quietly for her voice to carry.

"There is nothing like it. Exploring the world, I mean." Ellis's expression softened, one corner of his mouth ticked upward. "Perhaps, one day—"

"Mr. Webb, you are under the mistletoe," declared an exuberant, familiar voice.

Jessica's head snapped around so quickly she was certain she did herself injury. Florence and Franklin stood several yards away, arm-in-arm, staring at Jessica and Ellis. And Florence's declaration, though not overly loud, had drawn the attention of others milling about in conversation on this side of the room.

A sinking sensation overtook Jessica's stomach as she

looked upward, and there she found the kissing ball she had made. The bit of greenery and ribbon, with white mistletoe berries, hung amid swaths of greenery and silver ribbon. It was nestled deep inside, making it difficult to see from anywhere but directly beneath it.

Her throat closed and her stomach rolled. Not again. She could not repeat what had happened years ago, when Ellis had made an excuse to walk away from her.

Except...Ellis wasn't making excuses.

"Come on, man. 'Tis tradition," Franklin cajoled.

"Go on and kiss her," one of their neighbors, a Mr. Claremoore, encouraged. His wife giggled and added her voice to his.

Jessica finally let herself look at Ellis, to find him glaring in the direction where his cousin stood. She could slip away. She could take three steps back and laugh at him, claiming he was too slow to win his kiss. Then it would be Ellis who looked foolish, not Jessica.

Except she couldn't move. And when his head turned, his gaze meeting hers again, heat filled her stomach and the whole room grew dark. She should tell him no. Say he didn't have to, before—

Too late.

Ellis bent his head and brushed his lips across hers. A short, beautiful kiss. Her first. His lips were warm and soft against hers, and then gone too soon. Before she could respond, before she could even take a breath, he whispered, "I'm sorry, Jess." Then Ellis turned away, and he addressed his next words to someone else. "There you are. The deed is done. Now, who is responsible for hiding that bit of mischief up there?"

Who, indeed? Jessica raised her gaze from the ground

to meet her sister's eyes. Yes. Florence winced guiltily. But it was Aunt Temperance who had brought them to stand beneath the mistletoe. The two of them had worked together to recreate the worst moment of Jessica's life.

Not that they knew of that moment.

Ellis turned around again, and the wink of a ruby in his cravat at last stirred her into motion. He wore the lion stickpin again. Its jaws open around a ruby. Its horrid little eyes glaring at her.

She stepped backward. "If you will excuse me. I—I must—" She had no excuse ready. Her quick mind and tongue failed her. She turned around and walked away without another word, angling her shoulders to slip through the crowds. She did not stop until she emerged into the corridor, and then she went down the hall. She passed a few neighbors who had sought the coolness away from the gallery. She walked deeper into the house until she vanished into the shadows of a private room, one without fire or candle lit. There she collapsed into a chair and sobbed.

A reluctant, apologetic kiss was far, far worse than no kiss at all.

DEAR ESTHER

Brookfield House, Hatfield
December 26th, 1815

My Dearest Esther,

I may have experienced a slight setback in my plans for my niece Jessica. As I told you before, Florence and her Mr. Thackery are well on their way to announcing an engagement. Theirs is an open, honest admiration for one another that I have every hope will blossom into love. They are quite secure—though I can scarcely take credit. All I have done is encourage Florence to act more often on her feelings. The girl is most subdued by nature.

But that is not the point of my letter. It is Jessica I worry over. My plan with the mistletoe went exactly as planned. I positioned the couple beneath the white berried plant, then stepped away. I signaled to Florence, who agreed to assist in this delicate operation. She and her Mr. Thackery approached and brought the attention of the surrounding guests to the situation. Mistletoe. A handsome young couple. Everything ought to have been perfect.

I expected the kiss to lead to looks of surprise between the couple. Perhaps even mutual understanding of all that they hide from one another. (I have certainly spied Mr. Webb looking after my Jessica with longing more than once.) Instead, my poor niece appeared wounded by the kiss as she would an arrow to the heart. Though not Cupid's arrow, given her reaction. She left the party and did not appear again. It is nearly time for breakfast—I can only hope she appears at the table so I might discover what her feelings are this morning.

Mr. Webb's reaction was even more confusing. From where I stood, he appeared angry. Perhaps even regretful as he bent to bestow that sweet token of affection on Jessica. He is an interesting gentleman. I cannot think of many words to describe him that do not sound like detractions. He is serious and stoic. But there is a pleasantness about him, too. Certainly, he is handsome. I think those more mature qualities of his would be an excellent match for my niece's playfulness. They would balance one another and grow more alike in the best of ways. Of this, I am convinced.

I must mend this tear in my plan, and I can only hope to bring these two to their senses before Mr. Webb leaves Hatfield for his next adventure. I would far prefer he go nowhere unless he takes my dear niece with him!

Your Affectionate Friend, etc.,

Temperance

CHAPTER 12

When Jessica fled, Ellis did the only thing a gentleman in his position could do. He stood his ground. Pursuing her would start all manner of gossip and speculation about the two of them. Something he knew Jessica would detest. Perhaps hate him for, though he hadn't been the one to place the mistletoe above them.

No, someone had ambushed them.

And given the way Miss Florence turned white as a sheet and grasped at Franklin's arm, Ellis had an idea of who had betrayed Jessica's trust. He did not glare at her. A gentleman did not glare at young ladies. But he addressed his comments to Franklin in an undertone, so his words would not carry beyond the three of them. "You know she detests me. I cannot think of anything more humiliating for her than enduring such public embarrassment."

Franklin swallowed. "It's only a bit of fun, Ellis. Everyone kisses under the mistletoe."

"She doesn't hate you," Florence said so quietly he

almost did not hear her. He had much rather launch into a lecture. Or punch Franklin in the nose.

He slowly turned his stare to Florence, who leaned into Franklin's shoulder for either protection or support. Wise of her. He had a lecture in mind for her, too. "She cannot stand to be in the same room as me without making her disgust known. I had hoped to change that over the course of Christmas, but I feel you have made it impossible."

Those who had watched the ill-fated kiss had drifted away, allowing Ellis to relax somewhat into the conversation. His eyes darted to the door Jessica had disappeared through, but he doubted he would see her return.

"But it's true." Her chin came up in a way that reminded Ellis of Jessica. "My sister has an odd way of showing it, but I do believe she admires you. Whenever there is word of your travels, she listens intently and asks questions. When you come to visit, she always wonders how often we will see you. She wishes for your attention, I think. Have you not seen a change in her behavior these last several days?"

"That has nothing to do with her feelings toward me." Admitting it smarted his pride, too. He looked upward at the mistletoe and frowned at it. "We are not a match for one another, Miss Florence. Whatever you might think."

Franklin opened his mouth to argue, but Ellis silenced him with a harsh glare.

"I am not alone in that idea." Florence's tone was tart. "Whatever my sister's feeling are at present, do *you* think yourself equal to her, sir?"

"No." Ellis stepped away. "She is by far my superior." He left them and avoided them the rest of the evening. Let them sit in their guilt. He cared not if they tried for their own mistletoe kiss. He doubted Jessica cared. Especially as she did not return that evening.

The next morning, at breakfast, Ellis read a letter from his mother. She shared all her plans for Christmas with cheerful words and looping, joyful handwriting. No one loved Christmas as much as his mother did, and she had taken up hostessing duties for many festive celebrations in Bath. At times, the guilt of being her only child gnawed at him. She surely would have loved to surround herself with children during these events. Yet for many years she either packed him off to be with his cousin—her dear sister's only child—or came with him. This year, surrounding herself with friends in Bath, would be a wonderful experience for her.

What she needed was grandchildren.

He folded up her letter and put it in his pocket.

An hour later found him with Mr. Thackery and his sons out in the cold. The Thackery men had a tradition they performed on Boxing Day. They drove four vehicles into the snow. Two sleighs, two carriages. They divided into teams of two, going through the neighborhood to all the best houses.

They gathered food, clothing, and donations of toys and other needful things. Then they took everything to the church, to leave on the pews inside, so those in need might come to find things for their families beneath the compassionate eye of the vicar.

Because Ellis drove a sleigh behind Franklin's carriage, he easily predicted their first stop.

Brookfield House.

The Nettle family always heaped wonderful things

into the carriage or sleigh. Most items they had purchased or commissioned to give away, rather than simply including cast-offs from their home. It was something Ellis had always admired about their family. He had seen evidence of Jessica's giving nature often. Her parents' example had likely given her an appreciation for showing that kindness to others, whether it was buying gingerbread to give to her father's tenant children or seeking one of the neighborhood widows after every church service to engage her in cheerful conversation.

They stopped before the beautiful old house, and the doors opened wide at once. Two footmen came out holding crates, and then the boys carrying folded blankets and coats. They went to Franklin's carriage. Ellis pulled his coat tighter about himself.

The ladies of the household, including Jessica, came out and went to the carriage, too. They carried baskets, likely filled with food and provisions, to help families stretch their stores through the winter months. Jessica looked his way once but turned away again before they made eye contact.

Mrs. Bolingbrooke came out of the house last of all, her terrier dancing around her feet as she carried a basket of her own. But she did not go to Franklin's carriage. She came to Ellis's sleigh.

He jumped out to accept her contribution.

"Here we are, young man. You will see to it that makes it safe and sound to the church, won't you?" She beamed up at him, as though not at all concerned with her part in the kissing debacle the evening before. Ellis could not resist smiling back at her. She reminded him so much of Jessica. "It is kind of you to join Mr. Thackery in this tradi-

tion. I understand it is one of long-standing in the neighborhood."

"I have always enjoyed the visits." He looked up to see
Miss Florence and Franklin engaged in conversation, the
other family members already returning inside the house.
Including Jessica, who walked stiffly and kept her head
turned decidedly forward. Away from him.

"Mr. Webb?"

He looked again at Mrs. Bolingbrooke to find her
studying him closely. "Yes, madam? How might I be of
service?"

"Young man." She canted her head to one side. "Why
do you think your kiss beneath the mistletoe wounded
Jessica so deeply?"

Ellis stepped back, bumping into the curving side of
the sleigh. "You must be mistaken—I am certain Jess—
Miss Nettle was unaffected. Perhaps she did not like being
the center of everyone's attention."

"No." She shook her head decidedly. "I have pondered
on it until the wee hours of the morning, up until this
exact moment. All I can think is that the moment last
night held more significance for my great-niece than I
realized. I charge you to think on it, sir. Perhaps you will
know what might have caused such a strong emotional
reaction to what was meant to be an inconsequential
moment." She peered at him carefully, then nodded. "You
will puzzle it out, I think." She looked down at her dog,
sitting happily at her feet.

A dog she had been worried would run away a few
days before.

"Come along, Mutton." She gave Ellis one last
measured glance, full of mischief. "We will see you again

soon, Mr. Webb." As she walked toward the door, Florence at last broke away from Franklin to return into the house.

Ellis followed Franklin to the next home, thinking all the while. Around them, the world was white and gray. The clouds overhead hung heavy with yet more snow.

In the world's silence, broken up only by the sound of horse hooves on the ground, Ellis's mind stretched backward in time. What, if not Jessica's professed dislike of him, would cause her pain?

His heart squeezed unpleasantly. Had he hurt her somehow? The kiss had been brief. He had even apologized, knowing she could not want him to touch her with his lips. Despite the fact that they had grown closer—that he had even entertained the idea of kissing her that day the dog had gone missing.

Then there was their dance, too. And every moment leading up to it, when she had teased and smiled, when she had put her hand in his. They had been moving away from antagonism and to friendship.

A friendship he dearly missed. Which was terribly unreasonable of him, given that their previous relationship had existed when Jessica was still no more than a child of fourteen. Although she had certainly aged when he'd seen her that Christmas. He hadn't come back that year for the summer. He'd been away, exploring the world. He'd thought himself so worldly.

Ellis cringed as he remembered how he had gawked at the world around him, only to come home to England and pretend himself superior to all his friends. Then he'd stayed with Franklin for Christmas, as always, and Jessica...

The horses slowed to take a curve in the road, and

snowflakes fell softly from the sky as they entered the drive for the next house.

Sweet little Jessica had shown the early signs of changing from girlhood to womanhood. She'd been so eager to hear his stories, too. He smiled to himself as he remembered how she had hung on every word. And he had drunk in the attention like an arrogant little fool.

His gaze rose to take in the tall oak trees lining the path, their branches bare except for bits of mistletoe. Cursed plant. Ruining everything the night before.

The memory cracked against his skull with the same force of a fallen branch. He sucked in a breath and let it out with a curse. Last night hadn't been the first time he'd stood beneath the mistletoe with Jessica Nettle. It had been the second.

They stopped, and people came pouring out of the house with baskets and bundles. But Ellis barely said a word to them. Within his memories, he scrambled to put all the bits and pieces together. And he hated the picture that formed.

A young Jessica, eagerly looking up at him when the mistletoe was discovered. And he, a ridiculous, snobbish fool, laughing and walking away from her. Because he was too mature for such things. Because she was only a child. A child who had looked at him with such adoration that he had not doubted her affection for him. He'd believed that one small snub to save face would not threaten her hero-worship. Except he'd come back the next summer to find her changed. Where once she had followed him with cheerful laughter, she scorned him and delighted in secreting cheese into his pockets and hiding eggs in his boots.

The snow continued its lazy drifting from sky to ground. House after house he visited with Franklin, the ice dangling from branches and rooftops nothing to the cold and dreadful realization running through his veins. Could the answer to Jessica's change in behavior be explained by so simple a thing?

A moment he counted as inconsequential...had she marked it as life altering?

They arrived at the church amid a thicker fall of snow and beneath a darker sky than when they had set out. The vicar stood at the church's door, rubbing his gloved hands together and peering up at the clouds.

The priest hurried to help them the moment the horses came to a stop. "We best be quick about this, Mr. Thackery. I have already sent your father and brothers on their way. We may have a blizzard building and ready to fall."

Ellis hadn't noticed the change in weather, but Franklin nodded grimly and began piling things into his arms. Ellis stacked several soft bundles atop a crate. "No one will come to the church today, I take it."

"One hopes not," the vicar said, taking a bushel of apples from the sleigh. "But I will leave the doors unlocked, and wood near the stove, in the event some poor soul has need enough to drive themselves here."

They said nothing more, concentrating their efforts on clearing out the sleigh and wagon. Then Franklin unhitched the horse from the wagon, tying its lead to the rear of the sleigh, which would travel better over the completely snow-covered roads. They started for home, sitting together on the bench, a blanket wrapped around their shoulders and another on their laps.

"Dashed weather," Franklin cursed. "We can hardly see in front of us, and it only falls faster." He had to raise his voice to be heard over the wind that had picked up.

"It's a risk, going the four miles back to Lamblyn Court." Ellis blinked rapidly to rid his eyelashes of snowflakes blowing into his face. The world was losing more color by the moment, the snow falling faster and thicker than before.

"To Brookfield House, then," Franklin said. "It is only half that distance."

"Your suggestion has nothing to do with the fact that Miss Florence will be there to offer sympathy for our plight?"

Franklin laughed, and the wind snatched the sound away. "We might not even make it that far, Ellis."

"We will." Ellis urged the horses onward, the sleigh bells on their harnesses shaking merrily. Yet the situation at hand settled heavily in his stomach, and he set his jaw with determination. If they did not make it to shelter, the outcome of their morning work would end most grimly.

Robert burst into the sitting room. Florence yelped and jabbed herself with her embroidery needle. Aunt Tempie startled awake from a doze, making her little dog bark excitedly. Jessica, for her part, lost her place reading and glared over her book to her eighteen-year-old brother.

"What has possessed you, Robert?" Mother demanded, dropping her knitting to her lap. "You gave us all a fright."

"Franklin and Mr. Webb are here," Robert said, practically bouncing on his feet. "They're frozen through. Father said to come to the study at once."

Mother rose, and Florence with her. Jessica braced her hands on the arms of her chair but did not rise. She would *not* dash off to see to their unexpected guests. Though one look out the window showed their dangerous plight. Wind batted snow into the glass, and she could not see even a single tree outside. The snow had painted the world over in white.

Still, she hesitated. Until the door clicked shut behind her brother, sister, and mother. Then she relaxed again into her chair. Or tried to. She felt as though every muscle in her body had turned to stone.

"Jessica." Aunt Temperance's eyebrows raised high upon her forehead, nearly reaching her graying curls. "You do not wish to learn what happened?"

"I am certain I will find out soon enough." Jessica released her hold on the arms of the furniture. She reached for her book, which she had dropped at some moment without realizing. "There is no use in all of us crowding the room. Mother and Florence will not need my help."

"Hm." The disapproval in that hum smote Jessica's conscience, but that only lasted a moment. Because she knew well enough that her great aunt's matchmaking schemes were at the heart of that feeling. Aunt Temperance confirmed that thought when she said, "I do not understand why you have such an aversion to that man one moment and you act as old friends another."

"We were friends when we were children." Jessica opened her book and tried to find her place. "A long time ago. Now, we tolerate one another."

"It seems to me that you tolerate him, but he genuinely likes you."

Jessica pretended to concentrate on her book, her eyes focusing on a single word on the page. "I would rather not discuss Mr. Webb." Making such a forthright statement to a woman of her aunt's age bordered on rudeness. But that did not stop Aunt Temperance.

"Has he done something so very terrible that you cannot forgive him, Jessica?"

She snapped the book shut, and a less-than-civil reply made it to the tip of her tongue before she saw her aunt's expression. Aunt Temperance did not appear calculating, as Jessica expected, but instead quite concerned. Her eyebrows were lowered, along with her chin, and she peered intently through her spectacles at her niece.

Her aunt continued speaking, a little gentler than before. "If he has hurt you in some way, I will say no more. I have no wish to cause you pain, my dear, by speaking of someone who has wronged you."

How easily Jessica might say that Ellis had done her harm or caused her enough misery that they should never speak his name again. It would be wrong to cast aspersion of any kind upon Ellis, though. Especially since the truth of the matter had settled firmly in her heart after his mistletoe kiss. The moment in time that had so defined her view of him for years had not—to him—signified in the slightest.

She had wasted her energy punishing a man who hadn't any idea of the wrong he had committed. And it was wrong of her to go on punishing him. "He has not hurt me, Aunt Tempie. Not knowingly, at least."

"I see." Her aunt scratched Mutton behind the ears,

watching Jessica with a thoughtful tilt to her head. "But he caused some harm *unknowingly*, it would seem."

Jessica hugged the closed book to her middle. "Yes."

Her aunt's expression softened, and she looked older than her years. "I am sorry, Jessica. Had I known or suspected your heart was already bruised, I never would have caused that scene with the mistletoe."

The apology, unexpected and sincere, warmed Jessica's heart and brought tears to her eyes again. "Thank you. Although, I must admit that you were rather clever." Her laugh sounded watery, but Jessica didn't care. "I did not suspect a thing until Franklin Thackery pointed out the mistletoe." As he had done years before. Her breath hitched with regret.

"I ought to stop meddling." Aunt Temperance sighed and leaned back in her chair. "I became carried away when I realized you were unhappy about your sister's attachment to Mr. Thackery."

With a wince, Jessica wrapped her shawl tighter about her shoulders. "I do not know why you are encouraging her. She is still a child in so many ways. And Franklin Thackery?" Jessica sniffed. "He is so easily flustered, and then so ridiculous. I have known him all my life, and I cannot see what about him would attract my sister."

Her aunt actually laughed, though not unkindly. "Isn't it fascinating that some people find things to love where we see only an old friend?" She turned to stare into the fire, her smile gentle. "Maybe you should ask Florence what it is she admires so about Mr. Thackery. Though I will warn you, dear." Her eyes twinkled, and she winked at Jessica. "Your sister's love is quite genuine. You will not talk her out of it."

Jessica's cheeks burned, and her stomach grew hot with shame. She had not once discussed Florence's feelings with Florence. Instead, she had decided what was best for her sister. Jessica, who had only been in love once and ruined everything with her childish behavior, had no right to judge her sister's heart. Perhaps she owed Florence an apology. She certainly owed one to Ellis for tormenting him over the course of so many summers and Christmases.

The door to the sitting room opened again, and Florence came inside. "Here you both are. Mother bid me tell you we are keeping Mr. Thackery and Mr. Webb overnight. The storm has grown too dangerous to send them home. In respect for their difficulty, we are having an early dinner this evening." Florence smiled brightly at them both and turned to go.

"Wait, Florence." Jessica rose to her feet, holding her hand out to her sister. "Do you have a moment? There is something I need to tell you. Or say to you." She darted a quick look to her aunt, whose proud smile gave Jessica a little more courage.

Aunt Temperance placed Mutton on the floor and then rose from her chair. "Excuse me, nieces. I think I will go say good afternoon to our guests." She left the room, while Florence came further in, a curious tilt to her lips.

"Is something the matter, Jessica?"

Jessica released her breath slowly, trying to steady her nerves. "I owe you an apology. I have behaved in a most unsisterly fashion, and it is time I tell you why."

The conversation which followed did not last long, and it ended with both sisters in an embrace as they tried to stifle their tears. To Jessica's relief, Florence wasn't angry. Indeed, Florence said so many times she did not blame Jessica for her feelings that Jessica's guilt lessened to near extinction.

"I have loved Franklin for months," Florence admitted with roses in her cheeks. "I did not think he noticed me at all. Not until two months ago, when we were both caught in the rain. At the bookshop."

"Two months ago?" Jessica's eyes went wide, and she lowered herself onto the couch. Ellis had thought the fateful bookshop meeting a part of Aunt Temperance's machinations. But no. Her sister and Franklin had begun their journey to courtship long before Aunt Temperance had arrived. "And you believe he feels the same?"

Florence sat down next to Jessica. "He has asked if he can speak to Father soon. I told him to wait until after Epiphany." She blushed more deeply. "I do not want all the attention of our neighbors on me at once."

"How wonderful for you." The joy she felt was both beautiful and painful. Her sister had found love and meant to marry Franklin. "I am glad you will be happy." Even if it meant being left behind.

"But what about you?" Florence took Jessica's hand in both of hers, an anxious smile on her face. "I thought for certain that you and Mr. Webb had started to explore an attraction."

Jessica forced herself to laugh as she shook her head. "No. Of course not. Do you not remember all the terrible things I have done to that gentleman? No. We merely shared a brief mutual distress that you and Mr. Thackery had formed an attachment. I think he is quite resigned to the two of you marrying, actually."

"I should hope so." Florence's nose wrinkled. "He is

Franklin's best friend, as well as his cousin. I need him to behave himself when he comes to visit in future." Then she stood and tugged Jessica along with her. "Come. We have settled matters between us, and now we must help our mother with our guests."

With a playful nudge of her sister's shoulder, Jessica said, "You only wish to spend more time with Franklin."

Though Florence giggled, she did not deny the accusation as she led Jessica from the room. Florence never guessed, either, how Jessica's heart launched into her throat with trepidation. Because she knew she could not simply pretend the past had never happened. No. She needed to find a moment to speak to Ellis in private, and then offer him her sincerest apology for her vindictive, childish behavior.

The thing that terrified her most about the idea? That she still harbored feelings for him, and he held such power over her heart without even knowing it.

CHAPTER 13

THE CLOCK UPON THE MANTEL CHIMED THE LATE HOUR, BUT Ellis alone noted the passing time. He sat in a chair, stockinged feet propped toward the fire, trying to puzzle out his time in Hatfield. His boots were elsewhere in the house, being dried and likely polished before being returned to him in the morning. There was something rather awful about not having on a pair of sturdy shoes when visiting someone's house. It made him feel vulnerable, which made him cross. As did his thoughts.

After mulling over both the past and present instances of standing beneath the mistletoe with Jessica, he had observed her all that day. She had not spoken to him directly, but he had caught her staring at him rather mournfully more than once.

When the men had risen from the dinner table to join the women, he had found her already gone to bed. Though he did not like to make assumptions, the situation read to him that Jessica wished to avoid him altogether. Which made his growing attraction to her rather inconvenient.

He grumbled and shifted, sliding down deeper into his chair and letting his shoulders sink into the cushion at his back.

He hadn't asked to care about Jessica. He didn't want to grow enamored of any woman. Not yet. Marriage meant tying himself to one place for the rest of his life, in most circumstances. Not every woman was like the intrepid Mrs. Bolingbrooke, willing to go on camel rides in Egypt and sail the Greek islands.

Jessica...she seemed willing to go on an adventure or two. Not with him, of course. But the time they had spent together this season had made him wonder—had brought him to think they might have something together. Friendship at the least. But he had, of late, entertained an idea of *more*.

The door to the study opened, letting cool air from the corridor into the room to tease at the fire. With his back to the intruder, Ellis growled out, "If you mean to coddle me, Frank, spare yourself the trouble and go back to bed." They had been given comfortable guest rooms for the night, but Ellis didn't think himself capable of sleep with his mind busier than a beehive.

"I have no intention of coddling you."

Ellis reacted to the sound of the feminine voice too quickly. His feet shifted forward on the stool and his back-side slid off the end of the chair, leaving him folded most uncomfortably on the floor between the two pieces of furniture. He glared with consternation from his bent knees to his feet—still on the stool. Then he swung his gaze upward. "Miss Nettle." What was he to say? "Please excuse my lack of propriety in our meeting like this."

A laugh swiftly dashed away the startled gasp she emitted. She covered her mouth. "Oh, dear. I did not mean to laugh." Then she laughed again and put her hand out to him. "Here, let me help you up." She still wore her dinner gown, though she had removed her gloves. Her eyes twinkled with mirth, yet her lips remained pressed together.

At least she was trying.

Ellis took her hand and nearly pulled her down to the floor with him. See if she found that funny. Especially if he next put his arm around her and kissed those pretty lips of hers. Instead, he took her hand and levered himself out of his predicament. Jess pulled, leaning all her weight backward and contributing enough force that he stumbled forward into her with a grunt.

His hands caught her waist and pulled her against him to keep her from falling, squeezing a startled gasp from her, and then both stumbled a step before they restored equilibrium. Ellis held perfectly still, breathing heavily, holding Jessica to his chest.

One of her hands was against his chest, and the other had gone around his waist. They stood, tangled together, and his heart careened beneath his ribs. Jessica lifted her chin, and he watched her throat contract with a swallow.

Her voice an octave lower than normal, she said, "This is not an auspicious start to our conversation." She did not move away from him or what anyone else might easily construe as a lover's embrace.

"Is it not?" He couldn't keep his foolish tongue from

quipping, "I find I am already most amenable to whatever it is you wish to say."

Her mouth popped open, and her eyes went as round as they had when he'd fallen. Then she laughed and pushed him away. "Ellis Webb, are you trying to scandalize me?"

Reluctantly, he uncurled his hands from her waist. He tucked the misbehaving appendages behind his back. "Not in the least." He stood with gentlemanly posture, his face a mask of indifference. "What may I do for you, Miss Nettle?"

She raised an eyebrow at him, then pointed down. "Where are your shoes?"

"Ah." He wiggled his toes reflexively. "In front of a fire somewhere, I think. Drying out." It was incredibly difficult to maintain any air of dignity without appropriate footwear. "Is that why you came to find me at—" He looked up at the clock and his eyebrows shot upward. "One o'clock in the morning."

Jessica shook her head and took another step back, her gaze darting to the open doorway. "No. I waited upstairs. Near the landing. I wanted to catch you alone, in the corridor perhaps. But you never came upstairs after dinner. I decided to find you. Because I must speak to you about something."

Ellis nodded as though he understood, but in reality he could not think why Jessica would bother with him when no one else was about. She had ignored him all day, it seemed. And she certainly hadn't spoken to him since the mistletoe incident. The *second* incident. Perhaps this was his chance to make things right.

"I must apologize—"

"Will you forgive me—"

Jessica had spoken at the same instant as he, and she stopped just as abruptly. She narrowed her eyes at him. "Why are *you* apologizing?"

His courage did not waver, but he did not mind another moment to collect himself. "Ladies first, my dear. What were you saying?"

For a moment, she appeared ready to argue with him. That familiar flame of mischief appeared in her blue-green eyes. Then she sighed and lowered her chin from its defiant angle to something more natural. "I wanted to ask your forgiveness. For startling you a moment ago, of course. But for my behavior these last several years." Even in the low light from the fire and candles, he saw her cheeks darken in a shameful blush. "I have been awful to you, playing juvenile pranks and making jokes at your expense. Always so pleased with my cleverness and wit, when in reality, I was only being immature and unkind." She lowered her gaze from his and linked her hands together before her as though in prayer. "Please forgive me, Mr. Webb—"

"Ellis." He relaxed his stance, and he did not hide his smile when she looked up at him. Relief poured through him, filling his lungs and veins, and when he took in another deep breath, something kindled in his heart. "Let us be Ellis and Jessica again, and all is forgiven."

"So easily?" she asked, and her eyes glimmered with something new. An emotion he did not immediately have a name for. "Thank you. Ellis."

"I suppose there is more. Although it isn't a condition to my forgiveness, I would be grateful if you would accept *my* apology." Ellis rubbed at the back of his neck. Then tucked his hand away so it would not continue to give away his nervousness. "I think I have owed it to you for many years. I only remembered this morning, to tell you the truth."

"You aren't making any sense. Remembered what this morning?"

He bit the insides of his cheek. "I was an unforgivably arrogant beast when I did not kiss you beneath the mistletoe the first time, Jess."

She stared at him in shock. "The first time?"

"All those years ago. You could not have been much over fourteen. I thought myself so above everyone—not just you. I promise. But I think it was you I hurt with my behavior." He wanted to touch her again. Hold her. Somehow show her how much he regretted those actions long ago. "Perhaps you don't even remember. But we were under the mistletoe together, and I laughed when someone suggested I kiss you. And then last evening, when I had the chance to kiss you again, I was so busy being annoyed with Franklin that I did not stop to consider your feelings before I reacted."

"I remember," she said, her voice as soft as the crackle of the fire. "You wore a silver waistcoat and your ruby lion stickpin. Just as you did last night."

Ellis's heart cracked at the pain in her voice. He had hurt her. As he suspected. "I am sorry, Jess. I was a foolish boy."

She shook her head. "You needn't apologize. It was so long ago. I am the one who took that single moment and turned it into a bitter feud. Thanks to that, I think you have more than paid for your small mistake." She turned toward the fire, her expression downcast.

"I wish we could put it all behind us, Jessica." Ellis studied her lovely profile. Everything from the light tips of her eyelashes to the stubborn tilt of her chin. She had grown remarkably beautiful since childhood. He hadn't had the bravery to notice before, given how much she seemed to hate him. But since his return to Hatfield this winter, she had granted him a chance to come closer to her again. Close enough to admire her intelligence and wit. Her kindness, too.

Somehow, he moved so they were standing near enough to touch. He did not remember stepping toward her. But he felt certain he would have noticed her moving toward him. She turned to look at him, her eyes full of questions.

"Can we pretend it never happened?" she asked softly.

"Starting tomorrow morning," he murmured, leaning in closer. "We can forget everything. If you want."

She tilted her chin up. "Tomorrow morning?" Her gaze flickered from his down to his lips and back again. "Not tonight?"

"Not tonight. Because I have one more thing I'd like to do. And if you want to forget all about it afterward..." Ellis put his hand lightly upon her neck, and his thumb grazed her lips. "May I, Jess? I did a poor job last evening."

She leaned closer and closed her eyes, granting him permission to kiss her once more. This kiss, though it was his third opportunity, was their first true kiss. With no prying eyes and no mistletoe, Ellis covered her lips with his and bade her forgive him without words.

And he dearly hoped she'd have no wish to forget this moment.

Jessica had imagined kissing Ellis. She had hated herself for it, too. But finally, here at last, he kissed her. Not a perfunctory ballroom kiss beneath a kissing ball, either. Instead, she received a full measure of his devotion. Her whole body came alive with sensation, with memorizing everything about this life-altering scene playing out between the two of them. His touch on her skin was gentle, cupping her face to guide her as his lips tentatively brushed hers. Then, as the kiss deepened, his other hand slid around her waist and brought her nearer.

Heart thrumming, Jessica put her hands against his chest. Not to push him away, but to feel the beat of his heart and the way his chest shuddered with a stolen breath between one kiss and the next. Not that she could really tell where one kiss ended and the next began.

Years of frustration, of wanting, came out in the way they held one another. Yet everything was tender. His lips lingering on hers, then trailing across her cheeks before he enfolded her completely in his arms and held her in a comforting embrace. She fit snugly against him. Her head tucked into his shoulder and beneath his chin perfectly, as though made to lock in place right there. He kept one arm around her waist, and the other hand brushed back her hair. The spiraling curls that framed her face were— apparently—a nuisance to him. He tucked them all behind her ear.

"Ellis." She drew in a deep breath, enjoying the scent of citrus and spice that seemed such a part of him. What could she say? Expressing her devotion to him after apologizing for making him miserable—kiss or no kiss—

would be absurd. They had to begin again. She could not simply pretend they had been friends all these years past and that one night of understanding was enough to move into a new relationship with him.

She gently pressed her palms against his chest, and Ellis released her with a reluctance that made her want to step immediately into his arms again. She gritted her teeth together and stood firm. She looked up at him, trying to disguise her longing with a teasing smile. "Now that all is forgiven, I had better leave."

He blinked at her, confusion pulling his brow into wrinkles. "Leave?"

"We are alone. In the middle of the night. And you have no shoes on," she stage-whispered, as though the last thing on her list was the most grievous of all crimes. "As neither of us wish to compromise the other, I must say goodnight."

He continued to stare at her as though uncomprehending. "I suppose I expected something more."

"Did you?" She took a step back. "Why?"

"That kiss." And though he touched his own lips with two fingers, hers buzzed in response.

"You said we are to forget about everything tomorrow morning." Reminding him of that caused an icy shiver to run through her blood.

"If that is what you want." His smile hitched upward, brokenly. "But you may think about it if you like, all the night long. I know I shall be."

Jessica did not dare stay another minute, lest she kiss him again. And again. One evening together in such a way would do damage to more than her reputation—it would wound her heart. Especially when he left again. Away on another adventure. Because he certainly could not feel for her what she did for him. And he would leave soon. He was always gone after Epiphany.

She had wasted too much time trying to spoil her sister's happiness. She had not planted enough seeds to harvest her own. She whirled around and fled the room without so much as a goodnight. He wasn't foolish enough to call after her, either.

But she did think about the kiss. All the night long, in the silence of her cold bedroom, she thought of him. The way he held her. The touch of his lips to hers. His voice whispering her name.

Morning came, and she stayed in her bed. She was too much of a coward to see him while surrounded by others. Surely, everyone would know. How could she or Ellis hide it? The moment she looked at him, she would blush and give everything away.

She told the maid she did not feel like going to breakfast. When her mother arrived shortly after to check on Jessica, she claimed a headache. Her mother went away again, and Florence was next to arrive with a tray bearing broth and weak tea. But it was Aunt Temperance, when she came to see Jessica near the noon hour, who announced that Mr. Thackery and Mr. Webb had left with horses and sleigh for home.

Jessica sat up in her bed, supported by cushions, with a blanket pulled up to her chin. "I hope they have a safe journey," she said, not meeting her great aunt's searching gaze.

"Two miles in sunshine is far different a matter than two miles in a blizzard." Her great aunt watched Jessica closely. "I suppose we will not see them again until New Year's Eve, at church."

Four days away. And most people in the neighborhood stayed at home on New Year's Eve. All manner of superstition surrounded the death of one year leading to the birth of another. Even numbers sat at tables. Doors were opened and shut at midnight. Maidens bathed their faces in ice-cold well water. And no one wanted a visitor to walk through their door until they were certain that visitor brought good luck with them. Most of it, Jessica knew, was harmless fun. But it meant not seeing Ellis for more than a moment or two after the vicar's sermonizing.

"Jessica?" her aunt said, as though calling Jessica from her thoughts. "Why do you look so melancholy? Are you truly ill?"

"I am tired of making mistakes." That was the only true thing she had probably said all morning. "It seemed better to stay abed this morning than risk another one."

"I cannot say I understand." Aunt Temperance rose and crossed the room to retrieve one of Jessica's shawls from her bureau. She brought it back and fussed a bit while she put it around Jessica's shoulders. "Mr. Webb asked after you at least three times before he left. He was all kind concern."

"That sounds like him." Jessica smiled, though the expression faded as quick as it came. She leaned against the headboard. "Did he say when he would leave again? Usually he goes away directly after Epiphany."

"Is that what all the fuss is about?" Aunt Temperance huffed and retook her seat. "That is still ten days away, my girl. That is more than enough time for the two of you to come to some sort of understanding."

Jessica's heart skipped in surprise. "Aunt Temperance, the things you say. I have no intention of coming to an *understanding* with that man."

"Really?" The old woman's eyes gleamed like an especially gleeful cat's. "I think he must feel quite the opposite, given my observation of him this morning. Which is interesting, given how little the two of you interacted last night at dinner. It is almost as though there was an entire conversation that took place between you I am not privy to." She raised her eyebrows suggestively.

With a forced laugh, Jessica sunk deeper into her bed. "I am certain you are imagining things, Aunt."

Her aunt tilted her chin down to peer over her spectacles at Jessica, skepticism etched in every gentle line of her face. "It may interest you to know that I am determined to match make only for those who wish to be matched. Now. Do you or do you not have an interest in Mr. Ellis Webb that goes beyond friendship?"

Although she would rather sheepishly decline her aunt's offer of help, Jessica ducked her head and released a pitiful laugh. "What am I supposed to do?"

"To start with, you should stop pretending to be ill." Aunt Florence came to her feet with a sprightliness even Jessica envied. She took the covers in hand and tossed them back, making Jessica squeal and pull her legs in beneath her gown. "Next, we must discuss how best you might make the gentleman aware of your interest without coming right out and asking him to court you. Though I suppose it would not shock him overmuch if you did, given your forthright nature."

"I would never!" Jessica came out of the bed, her bare feet touching the warm rug by her bed.

"And we should enlist your sister's help. Florence knows you best. She is bound to have ideas."

"Must we?" Jessica's question came out meekly.

"Yes. We must. Now, let us get busy, dear girl. Mr. Webb mustn't leave the county without first knowing how you feel."

Jessica sank back onto the edge of the bed. "I think he might already have some small idea."

Her aunt, who had been about to ring for a maid, slowly turned to Jessica. "And what, precisely, do you mean by that?"

Her cheeks heated to an unacceptable level. If she pressed the thermometer outside her window to her cheek, she knew it would glow red with rising mercury. "There may have been an incident last evening."

Aunt Temperance sat down, a shameless smirk upon her face. "Do tell, my dear. It can only help our cause."

Groaning, Jessica covered her face with her shawl and confided her secret to her aunt. Who seemed far less shocked than she ought to have, and far more pleased than Jessica would have guessed any respectable person to be when learning of young people kissing without an understanding. "Stuff and nonsense," Aunt Temperance said when Jessica protested her great-aunt's enthusiasm. "Do you think you are the only one to ever break a rule? And this one doesn't signify enough to lose your composure. Let it not happen again until he proposes, and all will be well."

"Proposes?" Jessica squeaked. "But—"

"I will hear no arguments against that as our goal. He is perfect for you, Jessica. I knew it the moment I saw the two of you together." She tapped her chin with one finger, then adjusted her spectacles. "And we will make certain he knows it, too."

Jessica gulped back her protests. And hoped Aunt Temperance was as good a matchmaker as she was an adventurer.

CHAPTER 14

IN A DRESS OF A BLUE SO LIGHT IT REMINDED JESSICA OF frost, she walked gracefully down the aisle at church. She came in last of her family, trailing her youngest brother. With her head down, and her white bonnet shielding part of her view, she did not know for certain that Ellis had already arrived until she was nearly upon the family pew. He was already looking at her—turned halfway around in his seat, in fact.

And oh, how handsome he looked. His dark hair waved across his forehead. The deep blue coat he wore made his brown eyes appear as dark and rich as chocolate.

Those eyes were focused solely on her, too.

Her heart fluttered, and by habit, she frowned, trying to crush the hope down where it had withered slowly over the years. Ellis's eyebrows pulled together, and he turned away before she corrected her mistake. She bit the inside of her cheek and turned her glare to her brother seated directly behind Ellis. Twelve-year-old Matthew tensed, his eyes going wide as he likely tried to think what he had done to earn his sister's glare.

Move, she mouthed and pointed down the pew. He jumped up and moved with too much haste, knocking into Henry and Robert before sitting on the other side of them. Jessica took his place, then leaned forward to catch his eye again. This time she whispered, "Thank you, Matthew."

All three brothers looked at her with confusion while Ellis stiffened in front of her. He turned just enough to look over his shoulder at her, and this time Jessica bestowed her largest smile upon him.

Jessica greeted him, keeping her voice low. "Good morning, Ellis."

Franklin, seated next to Ellis, heard and whirled about before his cousin could response. "Did you just call him Ellis?" he whispered loudly enough for most of the room to hear, had not Mrs. Lesley released a trumpeting sneeze at the same moment.

Although she wanted to sink into her seat and hide behind a hymnal, Jessica kept her gaze locked with Ellis. "I hope you are no worse the wear for your adventure a few days ago."

The puzzlement in his expression, coupled with his hesitant answer, nearly sent her diving for the book of songs. "I suppose not."

Clearly, Aunt Temperance had mistaken the matter when she'd said Ellis was interested in Jessica. Kiss or not. Or...well. There had been more than the one kiss. But maybe that's what men did. Maybe they kissed anyone who presented them with the opportunity. Maybe he had already forgotten all about their evening.

Blushing hotly, Jessica sank to the back of the pew. Franklin looked from her to Ellis, his lips twisted incredulously. He appeared ready to speak, but the vicar strode to the rostrum. Both men turned around, and though Jessica kept her head bowed, she was keenly aware of them nudging one another and whispering back and forth too quietly for her to hear what they said. It seemed Franklin did know how to speak discretely in public. She still caught a few words as the vicar made his opening remarks.

"We come at the end of this year in an attitude of reflection. What have we learned about ourselves?"

"—a complete imbecile—"

"Have we treated one another as our brother in the spirit?"

"—you never listen to me—"

"And as we look forward to a new year, filled with hope—"

"—take hold of yourself—"

"How will we be better? Will we give more to the poor? Show greater love in our homes?"

"—if you don't, so help me—"

"Let us pray."

The men in front of her went silent as the vicar prayed over those in the church, asking for blessings in their parish during the new year. Jessica didn't hear another whispered word between them, though she'd caught enough of the conversation to be curious. It took every ounce of her will to keep from shifting about in her seat like a nursery-aged girl rather than sit still and reverent as a young lady ought.

As the time drew near for the service to close, Jessica

darted a glance at the full pews and debated whether she could exit the church before Ellis turned around to speak to her again. Her courage had fled and withdrawing from the battlefield seemed the best option. Mrs. Goodwin hadn't yet returned from visiting her son, which meant she had hope of sneaking out without drawing too much notice.

Except that when she stood, Ellis darted out of his seat first and intercepted her at the aisle. With as stoic an expression as ever, Ellis bowed. Then offered his arm. "May I escort you to your family's carriage?"

"Thank you. Yes." Why did taking his arm this time feel so different from all those before? Anticipatory tingles traveled from the tips of her gloved fingers all the way to her toes, and her cheeks heated as he led her to the doors. Perhaps everyone watched. Or no one noticed. Either way, Jessica didn't care. For the first time in years, she had no thought for anyone except Ellis.

Before she knew it, they were outside in the cold. "I have been thinking," Ellis said, leading her down the cleared stone path to where the family carriage waited. "About the other night."

She couldn't help teasing him. It came as second nature, after so many years. "What an ungentlemanly thing to do, after promising me we would forget all about it."

He frowned in response, his eyebrows drawing together, but the grumpy expression did nothing to fool her. Jessica knew him too well. Knew all of his expressions as well as she knew her world geography. Because she had studied both excessively for far too long. "Do you wish me to admit that I have done the same?" she inquired with false innocence.

The crinkle at the corner of his eyes gave him away. "Only if it is the truth. I would have no lies or misunderstandings between us, Jessica. Not ever again."

Jessica stopped him at the stone wall between the churchyard and a row of carriages. Then tugged him aside, letting others behind them pass. She lifted her face, making certain he had an unimpeded view of her as she answered him. "I have thought of nothing except you," she whispered, "and that kiss. I could not forget. Could you?"

His breath left him in a puff of white fog, a strained laugh as choked as it was relieved. He pulled away from her and looked about them with consternation. "This is not the time or place for this conversation. Is it?"

She turned to see a small knot of people standing near, Mr. and Mrs. Bierce among them, the latter watching with raised eyebrows. Jessica bit her lip and looked up at Ellis again. She shook her head. "Likely not."

Ellis adjusted the angle of his hat upon his head, and for one delightful moment appeared frustrated. "When, then?" Before she could answer with another word of mischief, his eyes widened. "Franklin comes to your father tonight. Perhaps I will accompany him."

It was her turn to gasp. "Really? Tonight?"

"He thought it might be good luck to visit after midnight. You know. Superstition being what it is." Ellis grimaced, and Jessica darted a look to the front of the church where her family had finally emerged. Florence was on Franklin's arm, their parents behind them watching with satisfied smiles.

"You cannot possibly visit *me* while Franklin is asking

my father for Florence's hand in marriage." Jessica's heart-beat thundered in her ears, and she shuddered, though not at all from the cold. "You might create expectations."

Ellis lowered his voice so only she might hear its rumble. "I am well aware of that."

Her mouth popped open, but she closed it again. Then took a step back. "Ellis Webb, you cannot mean such a thing after I have tormented you for seven years. Surely, you need to take time to know your own mind."

A smile, crooked and more than a little devious, appeared on his face. "I think that is just why I need no time, Jess. I've seen the worst of you for seven years, and I am quite certain I can withstand the best, too." Then he took her gloved hand and bowed over it, right there where everyone in the neighborhood could see him show her such attention. Then he released her hand and walked away, shoulders squared and head held high.

Jessica blushed and covered her mouth, lest everyone hear her smothered laughter. Ellis had always shown himself to be absurdly tolerant of her pranks. He matched her wit for wit in conversation. He held her future happiness in his hands, she knew, though she had nearly ruined her chances with him. Thankfully, the man also had a forgiving heart.

And she would soon know for certain if they were a true match.

Ellis and Franklin left Lamblyn Court shortly before midnight. They traveled with no moon, but the light from the sleigh's lanterns reflected upon the snow. They did not take the road, but a more direct path over fields from one estate to another. And they did not say much. Franklin appeared ready to burst from happiness. Ellis was lost in his own thoughts.

He would enter the house first. Tradition held that a dark-haired visitor after midnight, the first in the new year, brought good luck. Especially if he bore the gifts Ellis had put in a small box. A coin for financial security, bread for a bountiful harvest, wine for good cheer, and coal for warmth of friends and family. Then he would walk from the front door through to the back, taking the troubles of the old year with him.

And he had the feeling that was when Jessica would find him for their conversation.

The rest of the family would be quite busy waiting for Franklin to exit Mr. Nettle's study with the news of an approved engagement. At least, he hoped they'd be too busy to eavesdrop on the conversation Ellis wanted to have with Jessica.

"Nearly there," Franklin murmured as they climbed another hill, the only sound for miles that of the sleigh bells on the horse's harness.

"Steady your nerves, Frank. In a short time, the Nettle family will toast your engagement."

Franklin nodded, the flicker of the lamps chasing shadows across his face. "I know. But that doesn't lessen this feeling. I am as nervous as a rabbit."

Though tempted to laugh, Ellis's nerves kept him sympathetic. He faced his own challenge that evening. Instead, he squeezed his cousin's shoulder. "Think only of Florence."

Ellis had been adventurous his whole life. Many

would not know it by looking at him, he knew. He possessed a serious nature. He studied things out carefully before acting on his desires. But that meant the first time he stepped on Greek soil, he had maps memorized and legends whirling in his head. Not that he was any less enthusiastic to explore. Only that he had a clear direction in which to proceed.

Just as clear in his thoughts were the next steps to take with Jessica, the only person in his life who had ever managed to surprise him out of composure. With her pranks, her wit, her laugh. Now that he saw her clearly, he did not mean to waste another moment without her.

Brookfield House appeared at a distance, every window in the house ablaze with light to welcome in the year 1816. A year in which he would embark on a new sort of adventure, a courtship with the woman who stole another piece of his heart every time she cast a smile in his direction.

CHAPTER 15

THE NETTLE FAMILY, AND AUNT TEMPERANCE, STOOD IN the house's entryway, along with the uppermost servants. They talked and laughed. The boys teased Florence, who blushed prettily as she pretended to ignore them. Everyone awaited Ellis and Franklin's arrival. Nothing about Franklin Thackery's proposal was a surprise, yet they would honor tradition.

Jessica stood at the back of the little crowd, watching her sister. The joy in Florence's eyes, the serenity of her smile, reassured Jessica once and for all. Her sister loved Franklin Thackery. Thankfully, she had also completely forgiven Jessica for her unkind thoughts about the match.

"I think I hear them," Henry said, and everyone hushed to listen. Sleigh bells jingled merrily outside, growing closer with speed. Then they heard the horses' hooves, and Franklin's commands to his animals.

The butler took position at the door. The housekeeper fussed with her cap. It would be her duty to show Ellis from front door to the back after he bestowed his gifts on the head of the household. Though some might think their traditions silly, Jessica took comfort in the familiar gestures of friendship and neighborly care. Throughout the neighborhood, dark-haired gentlemen would perform the same act as Ellis to show goodwill.

A knock sounded at the door. Jessica's heart lifted into her throat. The butler opened the door, and Ellis filled the doorway with his presence. His eyes sought her, she knew, and she ducked her head as she blushed.

"Who comes to our home?" her father asked, this piece of tradition their very own.

"A friend," Ellis answered, and a thrill ran down Jessica's spine before settling comfortably in her middle. "Bearing gifts for the new year."

"Come inside from the cold, friend." Her father greeted Ellis with a bow and then accepted gifts symbolizing warmth and prosperity for the year ahead. A year in which one of his daughters was certain to marry. Franklin entered after Ellis had come inside, and Florence went to greet him with a demure smile upon her face and stars in her eyes.

Jessica slipped through a doorway, and then another, until she gained the conservatory. There, she put on cloak, bonnet, and muff. She had secreted away the warm clothing behind a potted fern. Once dressed, she went out the door into the night. And around the house, to the back, where they would ask Ellis to exit the house to take the old year fully away, making room for the new.

She waited behind a hedge, her breath forming puffs of white. The snow piled around her on the garden walk glistened in the light from the house. The back doors to the garden opened, flooding the path in golden light. She could hear their housekeeper, Mrs. Robinson, speaking.

"You needn't be outside more than a moment, Mr. Webb."

The deep voice answered her calmly. "I think I might fancy a walk, Mrs. Robinson. If you will leave the door unlocked, I will come inside again directly."

"Of course, sir." The housekeeper managed not to sound too skeptical about a man wishing to walk about in a frozen garden after midnight.

They hadn't actually discussed meeting like this. Yet Jessica had known this would be the best moment for their private conversation. Somehow, they were of one thought on the matter.

When the door closed, darkness closing over the garden path once more, Jessica stepped out from behind the hedge. Ellis did not waste time in coming to her, his long stride purposeful. She lifted her chin and correctly anticipated the way he would greet her.

The kiss Ellis laid upon her forehead melted through her. Jessica closed her eyes, savoring the touch of his lips on her skin. She wanted to wrap her arms around his neck and return his token of affection with one of her own, but she had worn her muff for more reasons than one. She tucked her hands tighter inside the fur-lined accessory. Then opened her eyes and grinned up at him.

"Ellis. Did you miss me?"

"Terribly." His gloved hand cupped her cheek. "I suppose you did not miss me at all? While I spent my time counting the minutes until I could speak to you, you were likely making diabolical plans for my demise."

"Of course." She took one hand from her muff and

pretended to adjust his hat. "Do not think that because we now admit to liking one another that you are safe near me, sir. I intend to visit as much mischief upon you as ever." Then she adjusted the scarf around his neck. "It will keep things interesting between us until you leave again." She tried to sound cheerful. But her words fell flat.

"I have no intention of leaving this county, let alone the country, at present." He stayed close to her, the hem of her skirts brushing his boots. Entirely inappropriate, she knew. But she could not step away. Especially after that remarkable assertion.

Jessica studied him in the darkness, taking in the tilt of his chin, the furrow between his eyebrows. "Are you not off on some grand adventure again?"

"Perhaps in time. At present, I am in the middle of the greatest adventure of my life." His low tones blanketed her in warmth, but that was nothing to the searing heat of his next words. "I am in the midst of falling in love with you."

Tears sprung to her eyes, and her watery laugh pulled an answering chuckle from him. "Ellis. I have loved you half my life, it seems. But I was so terrible to you. How can you forgive that?"

"I think love forgives many things. And how could I not forgive you? My stupid pride started everything. Then I was never man enough to speak to you directly, to study the matter and find its cause." He gave up on propriety entirely, wrapping her in his arms and holding her close. Jessica laid her head upon his shoulder, the wool of his coat soft and warm against her cheek. "Will you allow me to court you? Properly. With your family and mine watching our every interaction, trying to hear our every whisper to each other. Will you, please, my darling Jess?"

"Yes." She closed her eyes and breathed in his heavenly scent, mingled with the cold air. It was twice as intoxicating as before. Her heart rejoiced, her head gave up on cautioning her feelings, and Jessica kissed him. They parted when she shivered, the cold having made its way through her warm skirts at last.

"Get back inside," he commanded, stepping away from her. "People will notice we are both missing soon."

"I am certain they have already," she said, teasing him. "You will have no choice but to wed me now, Ellis."

"That is the most pleasing threat I have ever received." He pointed down the path. "Off with you. I cannot go inside again until I know you are safely out of the cold."

She gave him one last saucy grin before scampering away, entering the house where she had exited, and shedding her winter clothing before making her appearance in the family sitting room. Cakes and coffee were laid out, and everyone had gathered near the hearth. She entered the room as her father invited Florence and Franklin to stand with him.

Ellis came through another door in time to lift a cup to toast the happy couple's betrothal. He still wore his hat, coat, and scarf. And Jessica stood near enough to hear when her Aunt Temperance spoke.

"What an unusual thing to find tucked into a gentleman's hat." She sipped her drink while Ellis raised his eyebrows at her, confused. But Aunt Temperance stood on her toes and gave him a kiss on the cheek. "There you are, young man. I assume that is what you are after." As she walked away, Ellis took off his hat.

Tucked in the thick band around its base was a sprig of mistletoe. Two pointed leaves and a clutch of white berries. He smiled and raised his gaze to meet Jessica's. His solemn expression broke with a wide grin, and Jessica knew he would retaliate this time.

She quite welcomed the renewal of their battles because each would end with the two of them on the same side from there on out.

DEAR ESTHER

Brookfield House, Hatfield
January 31st, 1816

Dearest Esther,

I never expected my time with my family to extend so long, but when not one wedding but two were announced by my dear nieces, I had to stay. I cannot take too much credit for my great-nieces finding their happiness, though I will take some. I am grateful that what experience I have benefited them.

I suppose I have learned a great deal, too. I have learned that the asking and receiving of forgiveness can make bonds of love stronger. I have learned that love comes in different ways, whether in the quiet of a book-shop or the storm of a young lady's broken heart.

I cannot wait to receive letters from you and our other friends to discover what lessons the old year left behind, and how many promises the new year has in store. I have every hope that we will come together in December of this year to share in each other's joys once more. This time apart has reaffirmed the importance of our friendship and the love we have for one another.

Here I am, growing sentimental. Attending two weddings will do that to a woman. Of course, there was talk of Jessica and Mr. Webb waiting another month to extend their courtship. But why wait on happiness? If I could have one more day with my beloved, I would take it. I told them, "Best not delay. Every moment you have together, you must take."

They are planning their first trip together as man and wife. I suggested Egypt.

I wish you well and happy, my dear friend. I look forward to being with you again soon.

Your affectionate friend,

Temperance Bolingbrooke

EPILOGUE

December 24th, 1821
Nearly Six Years Later

A LITTLE GIRL SKATED ACROSS THE POND, HOLDING TIGHT TO her father's hand. Her mother watched from the sleigh, a thick blanket covering her rounded stomach.

Ellis looked up and waved with his free hand, and their daughter looked up, too. She wobbled but grinned broadly. "Look at me, Mama!" she shouted.

Her uncles played ice hockey with the Thackerys.

"I see you, Hannah!" Jessica waved back enthusiastically. They had come home for Christmas, and Ellis had brought Hannah to the pond every day to teach her to ice skate. Today was the day Jessica was brought to see her daughter's progress.

Ellis's voice carried across the ice, though not his exact words. Hannah nodded, her little face taking on the same serious frown her father wore when he concentrated.

Jessica watched, holding her breath, as Ellis released their daughter's hand.

Jessica's eyes prickled with tears as her little girl darted forward on her own, arms held out for balance and skirts fluttering in her own breeze. She giggled as she turned and skated in a wide, wobbling circle. "I did it," she shouted. "Papa, I did it!"

Then she skated away to her Uncle Franklin and Aunt Florence, who skated with two little boys of their own.

Ellis watched, then turned and skated to the edge of the pond. His gaze captured Jessica's, full of love and devotion as always. "She did it," he said, and Jessica wiped at her eyes.

A short time later, they sat together in the sleigh. Driving to her childhood home. Hannah sat snuggled up against Jessica on one side, and Jess leaned against her husband's shoulder on the other.

"You will never find where I hid my kissing ball this year," she murmured.

Ellis chuckled. "I find it every year. I am beginning to think you put it in obvious places on purpose."

She scoffed. "Why would I do that? Do you think I like kissing you? Arrogant man."

"Mrs. Webb, I know for a fact that you *adore* kissing me."

Hannah giggled. "He's right, Mama. You kiss Papa all the time."

"Dear me. Have I two of you to contend with?" Jessica tickled her daughter's ribs, eliciting a giggle.

Ellis's hand found Jessica's. He wrapped his glove around her mitten, then kissed her forehead. "My darling, you have two of us on your side. Soon to be three of us."

The pride in his voice sent a thrill of delight through his wife.

"I love our life together. I love Hannah." She kissed her daughter's forehead. "I love this little one." She patted her coat above her stomach. "And I love you, Ellis Webb. Even if you misplace all your left shoes."

"I misplace them?" he countered, sounding indignant. "Madam, we both know that *you* are the culprit there."

"You cannot prove it." Jessica leaned against him again. The tricks and jests had not ended with their marriage, though they had certainly grown kinder and a great deal more amusing. Especially when she finally admitted her part in them. But Ellis had surprised her by enlisting Hannah to his side for his own kind-hearted pranks. The three of them spent more time laughing together than anything else.

And they had traveled. She had seen Egypt, and ridden a camel, before Hannah joined them. Then they visited Greece, France, Prussia, and Spain. With each new adventure, Jessica loved her husband more.

On their way home that afternoon, they passed beneath an oak tree, its branches bearing small clusters of mistletoe. Ellis stopped the sleigh beneath one patch of green and white just to kiss her again.

Jessica's heart belonged wholly to him and always would.

"I love you, Jess."

"I love you, too, Ellis."

"I love Christmas," Hannah announced.

Ellis laughed. "As do I, dear one. As do I."

❧

If you enjoyed this story of matchmaking and mistletoe, make certain to read the other books in this multi-author series. Next comes *A Tangled Wreath*, by Laura Beers.

If you enjoyed Sally Britton's Christmas Regency Romance, check out her other titles in the Amazon store.

A CHRISTMAS MATCH SERIES

A Wish for Father Christmas by Laura Rollins

A Sleigh Ride Kiss by Jen Geigle Johnson

A Yorkshire Carol by Jennie Goutet

A Mistletoe Mismatch by Sally Britton

A Tangled Wreath by Laura Beers

ALSO BY SALLY BRITTON

Castle Clairvoir Romances:

Mr. Gardiner and the Governess | A Companion for the Count

Sir Andrew and the Authoress

Hearts of Arizona Series:

Silver Dollar Duke | Copper for the Countess

The Inglewood Series:

Rescuing Lord Inglewood | Discovering Grace

Saving Miss Everly | Engaging Sir Isaac

Reforming Lord Neil

The Branches of Love Series:

Martha's Patience | The Social Tutor

The Gentleman Physician | His Bluestocking Bride

The Earl and His Lady | Miss Devon's Choice

Courting the Vicar's Daughter | Penny's Yuletide Wish

Stand Alone Romances:

The Captain and Miss Winter | His Unexpected Heiress

A Haunting at Havenwood | Her Unsuitable Match

An Unsuitable Suitor

ABOUT THE AUTHOR

Sally Britton, along with her husband, their four incredible children, their tabby Willow, and their dog named Izzie, live in Oklahoma. So far, they really like it there, even if the family will always consider Texas home.

Sally started writing her first story on her mother's electric typewriter when she was fourteen years old. Reading her way through Jane Austen, Louisa May Alcott, and Lucy Maud Montgomery, Sally decided to write about the complex world of centuries past.

Sally graduated from Brigham Young University in 2007 with a bachelor's in English. She met and married her husband not long after and started working on their happily ever after.

Vincent Van Gogh is attributed with the quote, "What is done in love is done well." Sally has taken that as her motto, writing stories where love is a choice.

All of Sally's published works are available on Amazon.com and you can connect with Sally and sign up for her newsletter on her website, AuthorSallyBritton.com.